Elderberry Days

SEASON OF JOY

BECKY DOUGHTY

~ ~ ~

Elderberry Days: Season of Joy

Published by BraveHearts Press

Author Information: BeckyDoughty.com

Cover design by Elizabeth Mackey Graphics

ISBN: 9781953347046

First Edition: August 2020

10 9 8 7 6 5 4 3 2

Contents

JANUARY

January 10th

Dear Mama,

I fell asleep thinking of you last night, and so you came to visit me in my dreams. You did not come alone.

Yesterday, I took down all the twinkle lights I'd strung back and forth across the patio, and the shadows of the winter night that had been kept at bay crept in around me, taking me by surprise. The darkness left me feeling rather bereft, a bit like a lost child, alone and small. When Christian arrived for dinner, he eyed the solitary glow of the porch light in its old-fashioned globe mounted above the door, and without a word, went about building us a grand fire in the stone pit on the patio. The weather cooperated, staying dry and crisp, and the smoke drifted up and away, leaving behind warmth and soft light and the fragrance of wood fire. We sat outside, bundled together in a blanket, talking of trivial things that belied the depth of what was happening between us. Christian stayed long past my witching hour, that moment each night when I'm brave enough to send him away without me, and I stood on the patio long after he was gone, unable to go inside, alone. Oh, how desperately ready I am to go with him. Even now, my heart feels large and clumsy in my chest, pressing painfully against my lungs at the thought of making a home with him again.

Home. I have thought of this place as home for a whole year now, this tiny cottage cradled against the bank of the wee stream burbling past my patio. (Burbling. Is that a word? If it isn't, it should be. It's very streamish.) Beneath a giant eucalyptus tree whose rustling branches sing green lullabies in the January breezes, Elderberry Croft has been my home for twelve timeless months.

Here, at The Coach House Trailer Park, this hidden sanctuary I stumbled upon in what must surely have been one of my darkest hours, I found a whole group of people just like me, afraid to live, afraid to move forward, resigned and waiting for it to all be over.

At first, it was enough to realize I didn't want that for them, and I determined to do everything I could while I was here to help them learn to breathe life in again. But in time, as I got to know each of my neighbors here, I realized I didn't want that for me, either. We were all desperate for miracles, and God brought them in basket loads.

Elderberry baskets, Mama. Like the ones you and I used to make together.

The "For Rent" sign was so small, I drove right by it, the awareness of it not registering until I was several blocks away. I wasn't looking for it—the notion of moving out hadn't even taken root until that moment—but as I followed Eddie Banks across the narrow bridge over the stream, I could feel myself already falling under the spell of the place. When I laid eyes on the forlorn little croft, tucked in behind the huge Coach House, I think my heart would have broken if it wasn't already in pieces. It seemed as hollowed-out and grief-stricken as I was, in spite of the stream burbling (that word—can't you just hear it?) along beside it and the lush vegetation embracing it. If a house could be a kindred spirit....

It was little more than a shack, really, slouching resignedly in the back corner of the park, waiting, biding its time, just like everyone else here. The front door, painted a surly green, hung crooked on its hinges, the bottom of it trimmed at a discernible angle to accommodate the slope of the floor. The butter colored paint on the siding was sun-faded and chalky to the touch, although only peeling in a few spots, and one of the windows had a screen missing. The painted eaves actually matched the color of the door, as did the narrow trim around the windows. Not completely abandoned, I realized, but in desperate need of a gentle hand.

I saw the fragile bones of something lovely in its brokenness, Mama, but it wasn't until I noticed the tree that I realized I was the one the little home was waiting for. An elderberry tree, perhaps a decade old, had somehow taken root and was thriving along the edge of the stream, just off the east end of the river rock patio. Did you plant it there for me?

I felt like Mother Goose's crooked man (a crooked woman), having walked a terribly crooked mile to get here, stumbling upon this little crooked house. Sans, of course, the crooked cat and mouse. (Although I did have a crooked tarantula come visit one day. I'll tell you about that another time.)

Last night, after Christian left, I stood on the patio in the dark, just listening to the stream, and grieving for the elderberry tree I must leave behind if I am to go home again.

Another goodbye. Why does love always require sacrifice?

And so I thought of you. Of elderberry trees and baskets overflowing with the bounty of a day spent with you; in the kitchen, in the garden, in the woods. A morning at the library, an afternoon at the farmers market, laundry day. I only remember your baskets being full, Mama. Were they ever empty? You always had something spilling out of them. Visiting days, oh, those were my favorite full basket days. Homemade bread and cookies for the Fontaines with all their kids, tea and scones for Mrs. Tupper, pie for Phil and Lisa and treats for their dogs.

I won Kathy and her dogs over with your peanut butter treats, by the way. She's a wonderful neighbor, I must say, always watching out for me, trading recipes and magazines and gardening tips with me. I wasn't so sure about her when I first moved in, though. She was very suspicious of me, standoffish, always watching me from behind her lace curtains. I'm pretty sure she even used a pair of binoculars to get a better look! So that first week, I stayed outside as much as I could, cleaning up around the yard, settling all my potted plants into their new homes, hanging lights and wind chimes and bird feeders, giving Kathy a good look at me. All the while, I was studying her as much as I could, too. She had this terrible cough—one that sounded a lot like Mrs. Tupper's when she overworked her poor old lungs—so she wasn't outside often, making it difficult to just strike up a neighborly chat with her about homemade cold and flu remedies. But I finally realized that the way to Kathy's heart (and lungs) was through her dogs. She came outside with them for a few minutes several times a day, and I could hear her talking to them the whole time, as though they were talking right back to her. Well, you know me, Mama. I love dogs. I love cats. I love anything with fur or feathers, right? And they seem to feel the same about me. So, I put together a twig basket for her filled with a batch of your elderberry tea and a baggie of dog treats, a couple of pretty mugs, and I went visiting, just like the old days. Worked like a charm.

Earlier this week, Kathy snapped at me when I showed up unannounced with a large batch of elderberry tea. I told her I'd heard her coughing and she rolled her eyes and told me to mind my own business. She took the tea, though, and I wasn't hurt. Not really. I know she's not angry with me, but only sad, because I'm leaving. We've become good friends this last year.

I found myself singing our song, "You Are My Sunshine," as I stood out there last night. Quietly, so Kathy wouldn't be more upset with me than she already was, and so Doc wouldn't worry. Just the chorus, though. I used to think it was such a sweet, if a bit sad, song, but I looked up the lyrics a few years ago. It's a stalker song, Mama. You and Daddy sang me a stalker song as a lullaby! The end of that verse? "But if you leave me to love another, you'll regret it all one day." It's just creepy.

Regardless, how I loved it when you sang to me. How your words, especially near the end, came out sounding a lot more like the wind in the eucalyptus leaves than human melody, but I knew as long as you kept singing, you kept breathing. And when you could sing no longer, I sang to you. You are my sunshine, my only sunshine.

And despite the rather twisted nature of the song (a crooked woman must sing a crooked song, right?), it was what I sang to Julian every night. There were times I could almost feel you there with us, singing along. It was his favorite, too, even in the womb. More often than not, it was the only thing that would calm him. Two o'clock in the morning, I'd sit in the huge beanbag chair with him and sing, soft and quiet, just like last night, so as not to wake Christian. Sometimes for hours, until Julian, stubborn as his daddy, drifted off, unable to keep those big green eyes open any longer.

And yes, Christian is far more stubborn than I am. Oh, how I wish you'd gotten to meet him. I wish you had been there for our wedding, for Daddy when I moved, for Julian's birth.

For Julian's birthday. We had only one with him.

For Julian's death.

There. I said it. Julian's death. Oh, Mama.

You came across the bridge last night, and you brought Julian with you. You two were out on a visiting day. You held his hand in one of yours, a basket, for once empty, in your other arm, and the two of you chattered like magpies all the way up the front steps to my crooked green door. I sat out on the edge of the patio, my feet in the water, and watched you two through the window as you began to fill your basket with my things. It took me several moments to realize what you were doing, and at first, when I tried to get up, the water clutched at my feet, and the periwinkle vines growing along the opposite bank wrapped leafy tendrils around my ankles, holding me there. Just before I panicked, I was free, and I hurried inside to stop you. You and Julian kept talking, as though I wasn't even there, packing up all my things and tucking them into the bottomless basket. I kept pulling stuff back out, but I couldn't keep up with the two of you, and I began to cry, begging you to let me stay with you both a little longer.

I woke myself up with my sobs, but as I lay there in the

dark, trying to breathe through my tear-stuffed nose, I realized I was okay. I'm still broken—maybe I'll always be—and, well, I know my jagged edges show, but I think I'm okay with that.

It was so good to see you, Mama. It's been so long since I've dreamed about you. Thank you for bringing Julian. I'm glad you have each other.

It's time, I know. It's time for me to pack my things and go home. I don't know who "they" are, Mama, but as sure as I'm breathing life in again, I know what they say to be true. Home is where the heart is.

Christian, he is the keeper of my heart. While we have each other, he is my home.

Willow's Elderberry Tea Blend (Bulk)

Ingredients
1 Cup Dried Elderberries
1 Cup Dried Elder Flowers
2 Tablespoon Dried Ginger Root (not powder)
2 Tablespoon Dried Lemon Rind
2 Cinnamon Sticks (broken into pieces)

Place all ingredients in a glass bowl and mix until evenly dispersed. Store in a labeled paper bag in a cool, dark place or in a refrigerator for up to one year. If you store this in a clear jar or plastic bag, make sure you use your tea within six months to ensure effectiveness. This recipe will make approximately 25-30 cups of hot tea.

To Brew:
Stir ingredients first, then put 1/2 cup of the herbal tea mix in a thermos, or in a tea diffuser if available. Pour 4-5 cups of boiling water over the top of the herbal tea mix and let it steep for 15 to 20 minutes. Strain, add HONEY to taste, and drink. If you prefer to steep your tea in a pan on the stove-top, keep your burner on simmer for 15 minutes. Makes approximately 4 - 5 cups of tea.

Options:
Use fresh ingredients whenever available, especially ginger root and lemon rind. I also like to use my cinnamon stick as a stirrer, rather than breaking it into the tea blend. Just remember; sometimes using fresh ingredients will require you to adjust your measurements. As long as your essential ingredients are included, let your taste buds do the rest

FEBRUARY

February 13th

Dear Mama,

I woke up today to only the scent of Christian lingering in the tousled blankets beside me. He told me last night that he'd be gone early, so I wasn't worried, but I drew his pillow to me, burying my face in it, breathing him in. I didn't realize how much I'd missed waking up in this bed until I was back here. I've heard it said (by "they" again) that the sense of smell has the longest memory, and I believe it. I don't think there's anything more familiar to me than the wood and spice and citrus from his aftershave mingled with the man-smell that's uniquely my husband. In some strange way, it always reminds me of Daddy, triggering childhood memories, but it's not exactly the same. No one else smells like Christian does to me.

I have lots on my plate today, but I'm sitting in the beanbag chair in Julian's room, drinking my coffee and writing to you. I don't know exactly why I've started writing these letters to you, Mama. It's not like I have your address in Heaven, and I know you have far better things to do in that crazy, glorious, breathtaking, magnificent, beyond-my-imagination place than look over my shoulder to read the words I'm writing (like climbing epic trees or herping with Julian—I bet the reptiles are incredible in Heaven!), but it gives *me* great comfort to see your name at the top of the page, to picture your face as you read my words, and to imagine what you might say in response to my babbling.

I don't come in here and hang out with Julian's stuff when Christian is home, mainly because we spend just about every moment together when he is here. But he watches me when I pass by this room, his face carefully blank. I see the tightening around the corners of his mouth, though, as though he's holding back words he knows won't help. But when I'm home alone, sometimes I just end up here.

I found Julian's baby monitor shoved into a shoebox on the top shelf of his closet—I don't remember doing that, so perhaps Christian did. Although he didn't change anything else in here, at least not that I can tell. I'm glad. I don't think I could have borne coming home to this room dismantled or empty. We'll do it together, Christian and me, when we're ready.

I set up the monitor right after I found it. As soon as Christian leaves in the morning, I clip the parent unit part of it to my pants as I work around the house and garden. Christian has had a whole year to accept the silence that comes out of this room, but I still need to turn the monitor on and listen. I'm not crazy, or depressed, or anything like that. I know I'll not hear Julian, but the static makes me feel connected to him somehow, just the same, as though the line isn't completely severed... I know you understand, Mama. Don't tell Christian. Not yet. He'll worry about me.

Sometimes being home is like what you see in the movies. The daylight shines into the rooms in a soft golden hue, the smell of coffee in the morning, clinking pots and pans and dishes because there's someone to cook for and eat with. Waking up in the middle of the night for a glass of water and not bothering to turn on the light because my feet know the way in the dark. I feel like I'm drifting in slow motion, touching surfaces and textures as familiar to me as the back of my hand, a smile of perfect contentment on my face.

Other times, it's as though I must use a wedge and mallet to force myself back into a space that has closed up in my absence. Like one of those dreams where you are trying to run or scream, but your legs are moving through quicksand and all that comes out is a whimper. Those are the days I want to go back to Elderberry Croft, to my sanctuary, back into hiding, back inside of me where I can take out my pain and nurture it, feed it. Shut out the world and everyone in it.

But I saw what that turning inward does to people. I wish you could meet Patti Davis. She reminds me a little of you. She has this poufy brown hair like yours, and she wears slips, too. But it's more about the way she looks at Richard these days. Something in her eyes makes me remember those moments I'd turn and catch you watching Daddy like that. I remember feeling like I should look away, but I couldn't.

Richard. He was in terrible shape when I first moved there. Physically, he was and still is a tragic tale walking, but that's not what I'm talking about. He was even more twisted and raw on the inside than he was on the outside. It was the saddest thing to see, Mama, and I couldn't sit by and do nothing. I just couldn't. But it wasn't purely selfless, the special Valentine's Day evening Ivan and I concocted for his parents. I knew it would be a dark day, indeed, for me, if I didn't do something.

Christian sent me a Valentine card but I knew I'd need substantial fortification to read it. And since I'm not really a drinker, I knew I needed fortification of another kind. So I baked and decorated and made plans with Ivan and we pulled off one of the most romantic nights ever for Richard and Patti. Oh my goodness, they were so cute! And when they drove off into the night in that limo, Ivan and I laughed about how we felt like proud parents sending the kids off to prom.

When they were gone, Ivan helped me clean up, then we sat outside together, bundled up against the dropping temperature in jackets, gloves, and the glow of success. We talked about Ivan's childhood, about how things had changed so dramatically after his father's accident, and although he'd already thanked me a thousand times for the little bit I contributed, I could tell he was thanking me again by opening up to me about those dark days. I really like the Davis family, Mama. They're all broken in one way or another, but they want to be healed, and I can totally relate to that.

When the words ran out, we were just fine with sitting there in silence together, listening to the sounds of the night around us, letting the fire burn down, until we heard the wheels of the limo on the gravel drive up front. Ivan hugged me tightly, then hurried back to his folks' place so he could be there to help them inside. Ivan. I pray for him all the time. What a wonderful young man he is.

I read Christian's card after Ivan was gone, with only the glimmer of those February embers on his slanted handwriting. He has such lovely penmanship for a man, and

I love that he's always hand-written his letters and cards to me. He wrote one of my favorite Thoreau quotes in the card, "There is no remedy for love, but to love more." And his own words, brief and simple, were as beautiful as his script. "I love you even more." You know, I thought by leaving I could somehow lessen our pain, but I know now that I only doubled it. How wrong I was. How patient (and stubborn) Christian was. Is. I think the apostle Paul must have known someone like Christian when he wrote 1 Corinthians 13, that passage about love. "Love bears all things, believes all things, hopes all things, endures all things."

I spoke to Patti yesterday. She called to thank me for that night—I can hardly believe it's been a year already—and to tell me Ivan has reserved the limo for them again for Valentine's Day. Richard and Ivan have everything planned and all she has to do is show up looking pretty, per Richard's request. I could practically feel the heat of her blush over the phone.

Tomorrow is Valentine's Day and I feel a bit like a blushing bride myself. Christian is taking the day off (which is why he's putting in extra hours today) and we've not made any plans for the day until dinner. We're cooking Italian together, something we love doing. Bruschetta, Zuppa Toscana (we use your crock pot for that), Chicken Marsala over made-from-scratch spinach tortellini. Yum. We'll finish off with butter cream Gelato drizzled with some of my elderberry pomegranate jelly. Yes, jelly. I made a batch over the weekend and it didn't set up. But it's so delicious, we're using it like syrup for pancakes, ice cream, and even on our granola instead of honey. We're also drinking the last of my elder flower cordial I made last year while at Elderberry Croft. It's the perfect complement to this Italian meal—we love it in sparkling water.

It's been raining a lot this month, which is really good for our neck of the woods. Drought is always a concern here in Midland and last year was a really dry year. Besides, I love the rain. I love working in the garden when it's raining (if it's not too cold), and I love hanging out inside in fuzzy sweaters and thick socks, a cup of hot tea in hand. But I think I might suggest we go somewhere in the morning, maybe to Heaps Peak Arboretum up off Rim of the World Highway. The dogwoods won't be in bloom yet, but this time of year, especially with these cold rains, we'll probably have the trails to ourselves. Coming home to the smell of that soup, hot baths, and a fire in the fireplace? Sounds pretty romantic to me.

Someone's at the door. I'll be back.

~ ~ ~

That was Christian on an early lunch break, or so he said at first. Pretty early for lunch; it was only 10:30! But he arrived about two minutes before Johnny showed up in his truck, the owner of our favorite nursery out in the canyon. They were delivering my Valentine's Day present... two gorgeous little elderberry trees, both just beginning to bloom. Johnny assured me that having two trees makes for much better pollination, and I'm hoping by next spring, they'll be producing enough flowers umbels that I can make some elder flower cordial from my own trees. Wouldn't that be wonderful?

And how romantic is it to have two of them in our garden? Christian and I are going to plant them together in the morning before we head up to the arboretum.

I kissed my husband long and sweetly before he left to go back to work. My coffee is growing cold in my cup, but I am loathe to take a sip and erase the taste of his mouth on mine. My lips feel bruised, like they're still getting accustomed to that kind of activity after going so long without. How did we survive so long not kissing? Without touching? Without being able to breathe in the fragrance of each other? I feel like an addict—but in the best of ways!—when I think about him. Like the Shulamite woman in Song of Solomon, "Let him kiss me with the kisses of his mouth, for thy love is sweeter than wine."

Oh, Mama. A year ago, not only did I feel completely shattered, but I didn't know where any of my broken pieces were. These days, I feel like I'm finding those pieces, one at a time. I don't know if I'll ever be able to put them back together again (Humpty, you and me both), but at least it no longer feels like they're lost forever, you know? And on days like this, when some of those pieces actually fit together and I can see parts of the pattern of who I am, who *we* are, who we'll *be*, I cup my hands and let them fill with hope.

Willow's Elderberry Pomegranate Jelly or Syrup

Ingredients
5 or 6 Jars (8-oz) and Lids
3 cups Fruit Juice (from 3-4 pounds fresh or frozen berries.)
¼ cup fresh Lemon Juice
1 Box Sure-Jell Fruit Pectin (Leave this out to make syrup)
1 Teaspoon Butter
4 Cups Sugar

Preparation
Prepare your jars and lids ahead of time. Wash jars, screw bands, and flat lid tops in hot, soapy water. Rinse carefully. Place jars on clean cookie sheet in a 250 degree oven until ready to use, and place lids in a clean bowl or pot. Bring a few quarts of water to a boil. Pour boiling water over lids, and leave them to sit in the water until needed. Bring water in water-canner or large stock pot to a boil, then turn to simmer.

If fresh, discard stems from elderberries and separate pomegranate from casings. Ratio of elderberries to pomegranate is 2:1. Rinse well in a colander. With a potato masher or hands (elderberry juice will stain your skin, so you may opt to use disposable gloves), crush the berries thoroughly, then place all in a saucepan. Cook on medium heat until juice starts to flow, stirring occasionally. Reduce heat to low, cover and simmer for 15 minutes, stirring occasionally. Place 3-4 layers of cheesecloth in a deep stock pot, and pour prepared fruit into cheesecloth. Tie the corners of the cheesecloth together and loop the bag of fruit over the handle of a wooden spoon balanced across the mouth of the pot so the fruit juice drains. Allow to hang until dripping stops, then squeeze gently.

Cooking Instructions
- Measure out 3 cups of juice into a 6- or 8-quart pan on high heat. If necessary, add up to a half cup of water to make 3 cups.
- Stir in 1/4 cup of lemon juice.
- Stir in pectin powder.
- Stir in butter when juice begins to foam.
- Bring mixture to a full rolling boil that does not stop bubbling when stirred. Stir constantly.
- Stir in sugar and return to a full rolling boil.
- Boil one more minute, stirring constantly.
- Remove from heat.
- Skim off any foam with a metal or wooden spoon.
- Ladle immediately into prepared jars, filling to within 1/4 inch of the top of the jars. Wipe jar rims and threads.
- Cover with 2-piece lids, screw bands on tightly.
- Place jars on a rack in a water-canner and turn water back up to boil. Water must cover the jars by 1-2 inches. Add more boiling water if necessary.
- Cover pot, bring to a full boil, and let boil for 5-8 minutes.
- Remove jars and place upright on a towel to cool completely.
- After jars are cool, check the seals by pressing the middles of the lids with your finger. If the lids pop back, the lids are not sealed and jelly will have to be refrigerated.

Willow's Elder Flower Cordial

Ingredients
2 ½ Cups Sugar
6 Cups of Boiling Water
4-5 Medium Lemons (washed well)
30 Large and YOUNG Elderberry flowerheads. (Be sure to pick these when the flowers are just opening, but have not started dropping petals or beginning to turn brown. If you pick the flowers too old, they have a bitter taste. Pick the flowers when you're ready to make your cordial—if the flowers are not used promptly, the aroma will become unpleasant. Shake them well to rid them of any insects. There is lots of pollen at this stage, but it does not stain.)
2 Ounces Citric Acid

Cooking Instructions
- In a large saucepan or Pyrex dish, pour boiling water of sugar and stir until sugar dissolves. Leave it to cool to room temperature.
- Zest the rind of the lemons with a fine grater, then thinly slice the lemons, adding both zest and slices to the room temperature sugar water.
- Add the citric acid, stir well.
- Add the elder flower heads, pressing down gently to make sure flowers are submerged.
- Cover the bowl with a clean towel and let sit for 48 - 72 hours, stirring about every 12 hours (once in the morning, once at night).
- Strain through sterilized muslin or cheese cloth (sterilize by swirling cloth in boiling water).Using a sterilized funnel (hot water method), pour strained syrup into

sterilized glass bottles (see jar preparation above).

- If you plan to use this within a few weeks, simply cap and store in a cool, dark place. Once opened, the cordial must be refrigerated.
- To store up to a year, freeze the cordial in plastic containers, or do a hot water bath (see hot water treatment above)

How to use

Elder flower cordial is a concentrate. Willow's favorite use of elder flower cordial is a refreshing drink, using an approximate ratio of 10:1 sparkling water to cordial. It also makes an excellent dessert topping or flavor in frosting, fillings, puddings, and more.

MARCH

March 15th

Dear Mama,

It's raining again. We've had so much rain this spring! It's wonderful, really—so good for our drought—but after nearly six weeks of ponderous, murky skies, I'm beginning to feel a little like Henny-Penny, "The sky is falling! The sky is falling!"

Sometimes when it rains, I think it might be God weeping over the condition of things here on earth. The news is full of terrible things happening every day: school shootings, terrorist attacks, religious persecution, child abuse, spousal abuse, political bashing... you can't turn on the television or get online without feeling assaulted.

But today, the rain feels rejuvenating; a harbinger of something else to come, but something good, something hopeful. As though the moment the sky clears, all will be revealed. If I sit really, really still, I can feel my heart thumping and maybe even hear my blood rushing through my veins. It's a rather delicious sensation. Expectant. Like that verse in Romans. (Oh, how I wish you'd had a chance to read The Message Bible with me, Mama. You would have loved it! It's such a contemporary poetic version of the Bible. Although, I suppose you've probably read it, haven't you? You probably have access to every version of the Bible ever written right there at your fingertips. Will you read it to Julian for me? I know he'd get a thrill out of God being "Captain of the Angel Armies." How epic is that!) Here's that passage from Romans.

This resurrection life you received from God is not a timid, grave-tending life. It's adventurously expectant, greeting God with a childlike "What's next, Papa?" God's Spirit touches our spirits and confirms who we really are.

Pretty cool, huh? Adventurously expectant. That's how I feel today. "What's next, Papa?" And I do sense the Holy Spirit working in our lives. I don't know how to explain it, because it's been a tough week, but I do feel confirmed, as though I am valued on a level I can't fully realize in this life.

We... dismantled? Cleaned out? Took apart? Packed up? What words do I use? Julian's room. The little rectangular box in our home that housed Julian's earthly belongings is empty. But the immeasurable chasm in my heart—the one that's connected to the bottomless pit in Christian's—is not empty. I thought it was for the longest time. But last week, as we were taking apart the crib together, and I was crying so hard I couldn't breathe through my nose, I told Christian that I felt like one of those Black Holes in space you read about. Empty. Nothing.

He smiled, his eyes bright with his own unshed tears, took the side rail from my hands, and pulled me close.

"Do you know what a Black Hole is?" His voice so close to my ear was raspy, the way it gets when he's allowing me to just cry without trying to fix things.

"A bottomless nothing. A blackness so black that no—"

He cut me off with a shake of his head, then handed me a tissue from one of the boxes on the windowsill (I'd stocked the room before we began). "No, Willow. A Black Hole is just the opposite. It's where so much *everything* is crammed into one place, creating a gravitational force so strong that *nothing* can escape it, not even light. That gives it the *appearance* of nothing, when in fact, it's an area that's immeasurably full." He cupped my face with both hands, brushing away my tears with his long thumbs. "You, my beautiful girl, are the Black Hole of all Black Holes."

I know. Don't worry. He promised not to make that my nickname. At least not in public.

I looked it up. He's right, Mama. All this love I have for Julian, all these memories and longings, this heartache and grief. I'd packed so much of it so tightly inside me that nothing was allowed to escape so I could enjoy even the miracle of him.

For the first time, I really gave myself permission to sort through the Julian boxes in my heart, not to grieve over his loss, but to find joy in the time we had with him. More pieces, Mama. I'm finding more of my pieces, and I'm seeing more of the person I'm supposed to be. The Holy Spirit is confirming who I really am.

So this morning, Christian and I made Greek yogurt donuts. Oh. My. Goodness. I pulled some frozen elderberries out and added them to half of the batter, along with a little almond extract. Christian prefers them without the fruit, but we took some over to share with Dad. He loves the elderberry donuts as much as I do, mainly because they remind us both so much of you.

I'm enjoying another one with a third cup of coffee while

I wait for Christian to get back from the hardware store. He's picking up supplies for our project today and I opted to stay here and prep the kitchen. And eat more donuts and have more coffee. Maybe that's why my heart rate is elevated, and my blood feels like it's thundering through my veins. Caffeine and sugar. Chemistry at its finest.

Speaking of science (Black Holes and chemistry and human anatomy and all), we've decided to convert the breakfast nook into a lab kitchen of sorts for me. Wait. Let me back up a little.

Remember Joe from Space #9? And his drop dead gorgeous wife, Vivien? Well, last month she asked me if I'd be willing to bake a few of my elderberry pastries and pies for a big fundraiser event she was helping to coordinate. They attend this church in Los Angeles that has a really active homeless outreach, and they needed donations for a cake walk. Have you ever done one of those? I had no clue what it was, so Vivien told me it was like a combination of musical chairs and bingo, depending on who was organizing the game. I still have no clue—hee! But I'm happy to contribute anyway.

Anyway, Vivien was going on and on about how much people loved my desserts and how I should figure out a way to package and sell them, blah, blah, blah. Well, the notion got stuck in my craw (what *is* a craw???) for a few days, and when I mentioned it to Christian, he was all over that. He suggested I start with Mama Dosh and the Sienna Cafe.

I actually flinched when he said her name, at the thought of contacting her. I didn't realize. I just didn't realize. All this time, I've been connecting that day, that moment of neglect on my part, that selfish desire to look good at my own goodbye party. I've been connecting it to her. In some closed-up corner of my heart, I've been harboring anger, and bitterness toward Mama Dosh. If only she hadn't forced me to quit my job. If only she hadn't told me to go home and love on my child. If only she hadn't planned a goodbye party for me. If only, if only, if only.

Do you know what Christian admitted to me then? He'd eaten there almost every morning last year, that it made him feel closer to me somehow, knowing how much I loved that place and Gus and Mama Dosh. She asked about me every day and I couldn't bear even the thought of her.

How wretched a human being am I? Why do we blame those we love for our own failings? I was so ashamed.

Well, I baked up a storm for a few days, gathered my courage and humility around me like armor, filled a twig basket with elderberry muffins, elderberry donuts, elderberry banana bread, and individual elderberry apple crisp pies (cutest things ever!), all individually wrapped in pretty cellophane and adorned with handmade Elderberry Croft labels, and paid her a long overdue visit.

And you won't believe it! Not only did she forgive me (I told her about my shriveled up heart) and love on me (like the Grinch, my heart grew three sizes that day) and brew me the best Chai latte I've had in my entire life, but she told me that if I get a Class B license, something required for me to sell my homemade products to any retail site, she'll sell anything I can produce under my Elderberry Croft label.

That means my kitchen has to meet some rather strict standards, so I have my work cut out for me in the next few months. Although Christian's job is a good one, we're still living under some pretty huge school loans, so we've decided to do as much of the work as we can ourselves. Besides, right now, it feels good to have a project to work on together during this stage in our "sorting things out." A like-minded goal, you know? Something completely separate from Julian, or even from us reunited as a couple again, but still something that's an investment in our future. Something we can do side-by-side rather than facing each other. Does that make sense?

Oh, Mama. All that baking I did last year! All those scones and donuts and muffins and pies and jams and tea. Even the lotion and salve. I was frantically keeping my hands busy, keeping my mind occupied, trying to help others who were as stuck as I so I wouldn't have time to stop long enough to see how messed up I was. And now, it's all making sense. More pieces coming together. More confirmation.

And Julian's room? We're leaving it empty for now. We haven't really talked about another baby yet; it's still too soon, I think, but we've got time to figure out what comes next.

But the room does look awfully lonely now. Waiting. Expectant.

I love you, Mama. I miss you and Julian both so much. I still get sad. Sometimes I think I might die from the pain when it catches me off guard. But I'm not grave-tending anymore. I'm choosing to look for the wonder and beauty in my memories, even if I have to wade through the sadness to get to it. I'm choosing to be expectant, to look for the next adventure ahead of us.

Oh! I hear Christian! He's bringing home the new counter top we ordered last week!

~ ~ ~

P.S. I looked it up. A craw is the crop of a bird. It's like a first stomach where the digestion begins to take place in lieu of chewing, since birds don't have teeth. The bug or slug or grain or kernel sits in there and digestive juices begin to break it down until it's ready for the gizzard. We had chickens, Mama. Did I know this? I saw pictures on the internet of what happens when something gets stuck in a craw. I know there's no sickness or gross stuff up there, but if you have access to the internet, don't look it up. I am traumatized by this. I will never talk about anything getting stuck in my craw again.

Willow's Greek Yogurt Elderberry Donuts

Ingredients
2 ¼ Cups All-Purpose Flour
1½ Teaspoons Baking Powder
1 Teaspoon Salt
½ Teaspoon Ground Nutmeg
½ Cup White Sugar
2 Tablespoons Shortening
2 Large Egg Yolks
½ Teaspoon Almond Extract
2/3 Cup Vanilla Greek Yogurt
Oil for frying
Wooden chopsticks for working with donuts in hot oil

Cooking Instructions:
- Mix dry ingredients and set aside.
- In a mixer or a metal bowl, mix the sugar and shortening for about at least a minute on low. Add the egg yolks and mix for another minute on medium speed. Scrape sides of bowl to make sure batter is well-blended.
- Add dry ingredients and yogurt, alternating a little at a time on low speed just until combined. Dough will be very sticky.
- Cover to the wet ingredients ALTERNATING between yogurt. So basically, 1/3 third of the flour mixture, then 1/2 of the yogurt, 1/3 flour, 1/2 yogurt, and end with the last third of the flour mixture. Combine on low speed until just combined. It will be a sticky dough.
- Cover bowl with plastic wrap and refrigerate for at least 45 minutes.
- In a deep frying pan or large pot, heat oil to 325 degrees.

Oil must be deep enough to fry donuts in.

- While oil is heating, roll out the chilled dough on a floured surface to about 1/2" thickness. Cut donut shapes with donut cutter or two different sized glasses. I use a tumbler and a champagne flute.
- If you do not want donut holes, you can roll them out and cut more donuts.
- When oil reaches 325 degrees, add donuts to the hot oil a few at a time.
- Once the donuts float, let them fry for 60 seconds and then gently flip them over, using the wooden chopsticks to maneuver. Fry for another 60-90 seconds until golden brown and slightly cracked. Then flip and fry the first side once more, if necessary. Do not let oil get too hot or donuts will cook too quickly and be doughy on the inside.
- Place donuts to drain on cookie racks over paper towels.

Glaze Ingredients
- Mix glaze ingredients together and drizzle over donuts.
- 2 Cups Powdered Sugar
- 3 Tablespoons Elderberry Syrup or Jelly (February recipe)
- ¼ Cup Milk (depending on how thin you want it)
- 1 Teaspoon Vanilla
- 1 Teaspoon Lemon Juice

APRIL

April 25th

Dear Mama,

So I'm writing to you from my completely discombobulated (love that word— reminds me of the three fairies in Sleeping Beauty. They were truly discombobulated without their magic, weren't they?) kitchen. I have company. A wee little one curled up on my lap.

She has the tiniest ears, the greenest eyes you've ever seen, and a belly so round she looks like she swallowed a water balloon.

Against my better judgment, I am the absolutely smitten mother of a kitten.

Shelly Little comes by to visit me every other Friday morning, at 9:30 sharp, on her way to the grocery store. I make my elderberry muffins and she brings jasmine tea.

That girl. Slowly, but surely, she's beginning to talk about her past, and it's heartbreaking. Her father was a horrible man, Mama. I can't even imagine how she lived day in and day out under such a dark cloud of fear. Her obsessive compulsive behavior is better, but she's had to break those patterns ever so slowly, one at a time. Last week when she was here, she told me that she can leave her house now without going into a sheer panic that she'd left her front door unlocked while she was gone. I know the irrational panic comes with the disorder, but I wanted her to talk about it, to get it completely out on the table since she seemed so proud of it. So I asked her what she was afraid would happen if the door had been unlocked.

After three (I counted them) gulping swallows of tea, she told me she used to be afraid her father would come home if she left the door unlocked. I didn't say anything, but her father is dead. He has been for several years. "I know it doesn't make sense in the real world," she explained, her deep eyes flickering with shadows. "But in here," she pointed at her temple, "and in here," she put a hand over her heart, "it makes perfect sense."

I understand. Julian and you are just as alive today in my head and heart as her father is in hers.

A few weeks ago when she was here, Shelly also brought Bagheera. Yes, Bagheera. This tiny ball of black fur with her glass-green eyes is named Bagheera. I know. Bagheera is a boy name. But she sleeps just like the panther does in Jungle Book, her front paws crossed under her chin, her head slightly cocked to one side, her back legs bent up on either side of her body.

Christian calls her Baggy. Poor little thing. Bagheera, not Christian.

Shelly explained to me that the kitten had been brought to her by Eddie, of all people. He'd discovered the litter in the crawlspace under the big house at the trailer park. There were only three kittens, but the mother was obviously feral, hissing and snarling at him every time he tried to get close, and the crawlspace, although larger than some, didn't leave much room for evading angry mama claws. So, he decided to wait a week or two and see if they took off on their own. One day, when he poked his head under to check on them, there was only one tiny kitten in the little bed of rags and debris. Obviously the mother cat was moving the litter. But the next day, the kitten was still there, and from what he could tell, wasn't doing well.

Not knowing what else to do, he brought the kitten to Shelly. She was certain it was a runt, most likely abandoned by the mother, and she began caring for it. However, Eddie told her in no uncertain terms, that she was at her park limit on pets, and he could not make an exception for her, regardless of his personal feelings for her, or everyone else would expect the same from him. She could care for it until it was old enough to find a permanent home, period.

Shelly didn't bring Bagheera for me. She brought her because the kitten was still not out of the woods and she didn't want to leave her alone for long periods of time. But I couldn't help myself. I scooped her up out of the carrier and tucked her up under my chin, and she started purring, a ridiculous ratcheting sound that vibrated against the underside of my jaw.

I saw something in Shelly's eyes at that moment, an odd mixture of grief and relief, and then she smiled. "Um, Willow?" Her voice was quiet, as always, but I could hear the ring of hope in her question. "Would you like to have the kitten?"

I pulled the cat away from neck and held it out in front of me, studying her. That was a mistake. How could I resist both Shelly *and* the kitten with their big orphan eyes, both staring up at me like I was the answer to their prayers?

Christian says I'm a pushover, but I'm not. I've said no to a lot of things in my day, but I can't explain it. Bagheera just belongs here. And she's doing beautifully. When I got her just over two weeks ago, I had to feed her with a bottle (Yes, they make kitten bottles! They're so tiny!) and special formula, and she had to eat about ten times a day! But she's grown so much and is now eating soft cat food and drinking her formula from a bowl. I just took her to Shelly's vet a few days ago, an elderly man named Dr. White, and he told me he thinks she's about six weeks old, even though she's very small, most certainly the runt of the litter. But he gave her a clean bill of health and told me I was a good little mother. I half expected him to pat me on the head or scratch behind me ears.

The only problem now? I can't have a cat in my kitchen, not if I'm going to pass inspections for licensing. What was I thinking?

But Christian has saved the day once again. He's added French doors to the kitchen design! It's a good idea, anyway, to be able to close off the kitchen from any "contamination" from the rest of the house, something that will look really good to inspectors determining if I meet licensing standards, and it will keep wee Miss Baggy off the counters. And French doors are so lovely.

And so expensive. Sigh. That puts things off a little longer. The budget is already stretched thin, and adding French doors means at least another month out. At this rate, I may not make my first sale until next year.

Speaking of doors, I know you'd ask if you were here. Julian's bedroom door is closed for now. I haven't been in there in three weeks, not since before Bagheera arrived. No, it doesn't really have anything to do with the cat. That was just

Divine timing, I suppose; God bringing me a little needy thing to pour myself into. It's just that now with the room empty, it feels strange to go in there. But we're not ready to turn it into something else yet, so... it's kinda in limbo, I guess.

Last night I dreamed about it, though. In my dream I could feel this frigid wind sweeping into our bedroom, and I was shivering, my teeth chattering. I got up to see where the wind came from. I was barefoot and only wearing a sleeveless nightgown that barely covered my knees. I couldn't find my robe anywhere, and searched frantically for a scarf, digging through drawer after drawer, and only finding shoes. I could see Christian's suit coat draped over the chair across the room, but I kept coming up with reasons why I shouldn't put it on. I tried to wrap my hair around me like a cape, but the wind kept whipping it away so that it flew out behind me. I tried to pull the blanket off the bed, but it was too heavy to lift. Finally, so cold my fingers and toes were going numb, I hobbled over and slipped into the coat. It was still warm from my husband's body but it smelled like Daddy. I sighed and dropped into the chair, relishing in the comfort it brought. Before long, though, the wind started up again, tugging on my hair like it was trying to get my attention. So I got up and followed it, letting it pull me along.

I ended up standing at Julian's closed bedroom door. It sounded like a gale force inside the room, a howling wind through eerie woods. In a panic, desperate to save Julian from that wild ferocity, I threw open the door and rushed inside. Instead of chaos, though, I was instantly surrounded by peace. Not complete silence, but gentle noise. Birds chirped a sweet song, a clock ticked somewhere, and I could hear the murmur of voices just far enough away I couldn't make out specific words. Remember that scene in Snow White when she'd run in a blind panic from the hunter, and the woods around her was filled with terror? Then she wakes up to find it's a beautiful day and she's surrounded, not by creeping, clawing creatures, but by baby animals and wildflowers?

I woke up to Christian pulling me up against him, his voice midnight-husky, murmuring an apology in my ear for stealing the blanket. The man had pulled the whole thing sideways off of me in his sleep, and I really was shivering!

But the spell of that dream hasn't yet broken, Mama. I haven't opened Julian's door today, and I'm not going to. I'm okay with it the way it is. At peace. It's not going anywhere and neither are we, so until we're ready to make some decisions about it, the door will likely stay closed. Christian agreed.

He brought me coffee in bed this morning and called me his Snow Queen, apologizing again for taking all the blankets. I assured him that the cold never bothered me anyway, and that I wasn't sorry at all. I'm too grateful for that little dream to be sorry.

I've mentioned Disney movies too many times in this letter, Mama, but they're on my mind today, because you're on my mind today. April is winding down and in about two weeks, it'll be Mother's Day and I don't know quite where I fit in the grand scheme of things. I know I'm a mother, no matter where Julian is, and I know you're my mother, no matter where you are, but where does that leave me? Maybe that's why I had that dream. For now, I just need to stop trying to figure it all out and let Christian cover me.

Remember how I used to make you act out those original Disney movies with me? Cinderella, Sleeping Beauty, Snow

White? You were the absolute best, most believable wicked stepmother/evil fairy/old hag in the world, and you made me feel like the most beautiful princess in the world. Thank you for being such a wonderful mom.

I called Daddy and made him sing Bare Necessities to me and Bagheera in his best Baloo voice. You made a pretty scary Shere Kahn, too, Mama. Your accent was perfect, even though your voice wasn't nearly deep enough.

I love you.

Willow's Elderberry Muffins

Batter Ingredients:
2 Cups Flour
2 Teaspoons Baking Powder
½ Teaspoon Salt
½ Cup Butter or Margarine (room temperature)
1 Cup Sugar
2 Eggs
1 Teaspoon Vanilla
½ Cup Milk
½ Cup Dried and Reconstituted Elderberries (instructions below) or 1 Cup Fresh Elderberries

Topping:
(Crumble all ingredients together with a fork, set aside.)
½ Cup White Sugar
½ Cup Brown Sugar
½ Cup All-Purpose Flour
¼ Cup Butter (softened, cubed)
2 Teaspoons Ground Cinnamon

Cooking Instructions:
(Reconstituting your berries: If elderberries are dry, cover ½ cup dried berries in boiling water, and let sit for 3 hours.)
- Preheat oven to 375 degrees.
- Grease 18 regular-size muffin cups or line with muffin papers (or 12 LARGE muffins).
- In a bowl, mix butter until creamy. Then mix in sugar until thick and fluffy. This is a very important step – mix it longer than you think you should. The ingredients should expand.

- Add eggs, one at a time, beating after each.
- Add milk and vanilla, mix well.
- In a separate bowl, thoroughly combine flour and baking powder, then fold in half at a time to wet ingredients. VERY IMPORTANT: Once baking powder gets wet, it begins to activate. DO NOT OVER MIX. Batter should be moist and lumpy – think oatmeal.
- Fold in elderberries (1 cup fresh, or the ½ cup reconstituted).Spoon into muffin tins, sprinkle with crumb topping.
- Bake approximately 20 minutes, or until toothpick inserted in thickest part of muffin comes out clean.

If elderberries aren't easily accessible, this makes a DELICIOUS berry-of-your-choice muffin recipe, too. It's *also* yummy with no fruit – just add some cinnamon to the batter for a little bit of flavor.

MAY

May 19th

Dear Mama,

Oh Mama. Last night I woke up from a sound sleep and I knew something was wasn't right. I lay there in the dark, wide-awake, my heart pounding so loudly it was all I could hear for a few moments. I had this strange superimposed memory from childhood, as though for just a split second, I actually was Miss Clavel in the orphanage in France, sitting up in the middle of the night, knowing something was not right.

I couldn't tell you what it was that woke me; Christian didn't stir beside me. But maybe that's why. He was so still, every muscle in his body rigid, not even breathing that I could tell. But when I reached for him, he flinched, and drew in a breath that made me think of a drowning man.

And then he started to tremble. The curve of his shoulder where I rested my hand was chilled, even under the covers, and a bit clammy, and the tiny muscles just beneath his skin twitched and flickered as though an electric current passed through him. I pushed up on my elbow, rolling toward him, trying not to panic.

"What's wrong?" My voice vibrated with fear.

He didn't answer, but the air he'd sucked in came back out in whoosh that turned into a sound as wretched as I'd ever heard come out of a human being.

"Oh, honey, Christian, honey, what is it?" I pulled him to me, and like a child, he burrowed his face into my chest, his long arms encircling me, clutching me tightly to him. And he wept in deep, gulping sobs, not loudly, but in such a way that left him lying spent in my embrace after only a few minutes.

I cried, too, in helplessness, not knowing how to give him comfort, not knowing what to say.

"Oh, God," he moaned, his voice muffled against the fabric of my pajama top. "Oh God, I'm sorry, Willow. I'm so sorry. I'm sorry."

"It's okay, honey. Shh. It's okay." But in that moment, I didn't know if it would ever be okay again.

We both needed a tissue, but I was afraid to move, to reach for the box on my nightstand. The night air seemed too thin to hold us together, and if one of us uncoiled an arm, we might slip apart and never find our way back to each other.

We lay there in the dark, drenched in tears and despair, out of time, out of place, until finally, Christian began to speak. Just a murmur at first, so low I couldn't make out individual words, but his voice was like a beacon, and I homed in on it, listening with my heart until I could understand what he said.

"I can't remember, Willow. I remember arguing with you about my shirt. I remember eating half the fried egg sandwich you made me, then setting aside the rest of it to take with me and finish in the truck on my way to work. I remember the television being on and coming around the corner to see Julian, fist full of crackers or cereal practically shoved into his mouth, hypnotized by whatever cartoon he watched. But I don't remember leaving the house. I don't remember walking out the door and not double-checking to make sure it latched behind me. I don't remember getting in the truck—" His voice broke off in a choked sob. "It's like those scenes in movies where everything slows down so much that the sound warps into a moaning or wailing, every movement and expression exposed and in clear focus. But in my mind, it's only sound. Everything just fades to black when I try to remember."

As long as he kept talking, I was tethered to him by the shredded strands of his voice; still fragile, but strong enough for me to grab the tissue box. I balanced the box on the curve of my hip, in easy reach for both of us. He plucked several out and shoved them up between his face and my shirt, blowing his nose only enough to be able to speak more clearly.

"I dream about that morning sometimes. It's the same thing every time. That fried egg sandwich, the television playing in the other room, ironing my shirt and angry at myself for being angry at you. It's like I'm right there all over again. But in my dream," his throat tightened and he swallowed hard. "I know what's going to happen, Willow. I know what's coming. And even though I know, I can't change anything. I can't stop eating that sandwich, and I can't go in the living room and pick Julian up and turn off the television, and I can't stop being angry at you, but I *know* if I don't, the blackness will come and consume us all. But I can't do anything different. I just watch myself do it all over again and again and again." The last words came out in tatters.

"Oh Christian. Oh, honey." Words failed me, and all I could do was offer what little comfort my presence was. I cupped the back of his head, my fingers buried in his soft short hair, pressing him to me. My heart beneath his cheek ached at the pain in his voice. Why had I never asked him how he was coping, how he was dealing? Why did I imagine, even for one moment, that my suffering was greater than his?

"It all goes black," he continued. "I can hear the distorted sound, but other than that, it's like I'm floating in space, completely adrift and alone in the blackness. Then, suddenly, everything sweeps back in and the wailing is you in my dream, and I wake up, my own moan stuck in my throat." Another tremor coursed through him.

I could hardly breathe, let alone say anything coherent. So much pain. So much suffering.

And I'd left him alone.

I'd abandoned him to the blackness.

"I think," his voice wasn't much more than a whisper, trembling, but brave. "I think—I think if I could remember what came next, I might stop dreaming about it." He ran his right hand absentmindedly up and down the curve of my back, fingering the knobs of my spine. His hold on me began to loosen so he wasn't quite clinging to me anymore, his body relaxing against mine.

"I didn't know, Christian," I finally whispered back. "Why didn't you tell me? I—you haven't—have you dreamed this since I've been home?" Was it possible he'd suffered like this in silence, lying beside me, trembling and weeping, without reaching out for me? I didn't know whether to be hurt, angry, or even more afraid for us.

"Not at first. In fact, I didn't dream about that day for nearly three months, and I thought maybe with you home, here with me, it had gone. But then," he sighed, his warm breath feathering across the sensitive skin over my collarbone where it was exposed at the edge of the neckline of my top. He'd turned his face away from my chest so he could breathe easier, so he could speak more freely. "But last month, after we put all Julian's things away—"

"Why didn't you wake me?" I spoke quietly, my words weighed down by grief, both mine and his.

I could feel him shake his head against my chest. "I didn't think—I didn't think—"

"You didn't think what? That I could handle it?" I tried not to let resentment creep into my voice, but I heard it anyway.

"No! No, Willow." He lifted his head for the first time, pulling away a little so he could look at me, his face only inches from mine. There wasn't enough light to make out much more than the silhouette of his rumpled hair and angular jaw line and the ridge of his straight nose, but I could feel his eyes searching for mine in the darkness. "I just assumed it had returned because we'd worked in his room, and because we talked so much about him, but that it would go away again. Apparently that's not quite the way it's going to be." He sighed deeply, and even though I sensed his discouragement, I also thought I heard a hint of relief in the telling.

"It's better, though, with you here." He lowered his head again and murmured against my neck.

Christian has been like this monument of strength to me this last year and a half. Always steadfast, always faithful, always there, even when I wasn't. I *needed* him to be a rock for us. I needed him to be immovable because I was on such shaky ground. I needed him to push through this, in order to prove to me it could be done. I needed to know that if I followed him, we'd get through this to the other side.

I didn't know. I didn't know how much he needed me, too.

Because I didn't ask. And because he didn't tell.

Oh, Mama. Will we ever be put back together again?

We didn't talk for a long time, but finally, my arm beneath him started tingling and I had to move. We eased apart just long enough for me to remove my damp shirt. Before I could get out of bed to find another one, he pulled me back up against him, and together, we searched for, and found, a few more of our broken pieces in the dark.

Before we fell asleep, we prayed together, asking God to cover our home, our room, our bed, to protect our sleep and our dreams. Christian shared something with me that I thought was so cool. In the Bible, there are so many verses that talk about being able to sleep in peace, to lie down and rest because God protects. But sometimes that seems so trite, because we know it isn't always like that. Sometimes we're attacked by fear and doubt and dark thoughts, and when we sleep, and those things come to us in our dreams, it's like being hit when we're at our most vulnerable.

So Christian told me about something he found in Psalm 59. He really likes the New King James Version Bible and in this section, King David is surrounded by his enemies and he cries out to God, *"For look, they lie in wait for my life; the mighty gather against me, not for my transgression nor of my sin, O Lord. They run and prepare themselves through no fault of mine. Awake to help me, and behold! You therefore, O Lord God of hosts, the God of Israel. Awake to punish all the nations; Do not be merciful to any wicked transgressions."*

I looked it up in my Message Bible today, just to see what

it said. Check this out. "Desperadoes have ganged up on me, they're hiding in ambush for me. I did nothing to deserve this, God, crossed no one, wronged no one. All the same, they're after me, determined to get me. Wake up and see for yourself! You're GOD, God-of-Angel-Armies, Israel's God! Get on the job and take care of these pagans, don't be soft on these hard cases."

Okay. At first glance, I know that may seem presumptuous of David, demanding that God wake up and show up, but the more I read through Chapter 59, the more I realized David was not really ordering God around, but rather, he was reminding himself that God was not only awake and aware, but beyond capable of crushing the bad guys because God was—and is!—Lord of hosts, God of Angel Armies! David's cry wasn't one of *unbelief*, but that of a beloved child, waking up in the middle of the night, caught in the throes of terror, and calling out, in spite of his fear, *believing* his father would show up. David knew God was there, and He would show up, and He would bring with Him that peace that would allow him to lay his head down again and rest.

And that's what Christian clings to, that desperate cry of anguished *belief* that God will and does show up, even in the dead of night when everyone else is asleep. He says the verses feel active, not passive, like he's able to do something rather than just lying there in the dark waiting for the undisturbed sleep that believers are supposedly blessed with. Ha! He says it's like swinging a sword instead, like charging in with the mightiest of all armies. I think I understand.

So we prayed David's prayer together last night. Awake to help us. You are God. You are God of Angel Armies.

And we slept. In each other's arms, and in peace.

There was something else in that passage that did my heart good to hear, Mama. The part where David says, "I did nothing to deserve this." Christian and I *did* do something to deserve this, and we're both well aware of it. But somehow, we're learning to forgive ourselves, and each other, and to accept the forgiveness and mercy God offers us. David was no saint either, but he knew he was living freely under the covering of God, and could call on Him at any time. We're learning to live under that same covering.

Will the dream keep coming back? Will Christian remember? *Should* he remember those terrible moments? I don't know. But I feel like we're armed and ready for whatever comes, and leading the charge is the God of Israel, the Lord of hosts, the God of the Angel Armies.

Despair turns to fragile hope yet again.

Tomorrow is Christian's birthday. He's asked me to make your cheesecake, Mama. It's what he asks for every year. And that elderberry-pomegranate jelly-turned-syrup? I'm going to toss a few blueberries into it and drizzle it over the top to class it up a little. Doesn't that sound scrumptious?

We're holding on to every extra dollar to put into the kitchen remodel—everything costs a little more than we'd planned, and takes a little longer than we'd planned, but it's coming together. Our goal is to have it ready for me to make my first batch of scones by my birthday next month. The remodel won't be finished, but I'll be able to start using that side of the kitchen again.

In other words, we're not going to do anything that costs too much for either of our birthdays this year. I'm cooking a pot roast for him—his favorite home-cooked meal of all time—and we're watching a movie of his choice here at home. With freshly-popped popcorn, the real deal, the kind you pop in a big pot on the stove top. He loves the real deal popcorn. Loves it. Can't stand to sit down to watch a movie until he's popped a batch of popcorn and drenched it in melted butter and tossed it with too much salt. It's part of the movie night ritual in our home.

I love this man God gave me, Mama. And I feel like I'm blooming again, like my happy plants are doing out back, in the love that he has for me. We're getting better. It's not easy, but we're getting better at moving forward. I'm just glad I'm here to celebrate Christian this year (I'm ashamed to admit I didn't even send him a card last year), not just because it's his birthday, but because every new day we have together is a reason to celebrate. We're learning to find joy in both big and little things, and that joy inspires hope.

Princess Baggy waves a teeny tiny paw at you and Julian, Mama. Are there kittens in Heaven?

Christian's Birthday Cheesecake

Ingredients
2 8-oz Packages of Cream Cheese (softened)
1 Cup White Sugar
2 Eggs
1 Teaspoon Vanilla Extract
1 Teaspoon Almond Extract
1 Cup Sour Cream
Fresh Raspberries, Blueberries, Boysenberries, and Elderberries
Elderberry Syrup

Graham cracker crust
1 ½ Cups Graham Cracker Crumbs
½ Cup Butter
¼ Cup Sugar

Cooking Instructions:
- Preheat oven to 350 degrees.
- Mix graham cracker crust ingredients and press evenly into the bottom of a 9-inch spring-form pan of a 9- inch round cake pan.
- Bake for 8 to 10 minutes, set on wire rack to cool completely.
- IMPORTANT: Turn oven down to 325 degrees for cheesecake.
- Cream together cream cheese and sugar.
- Add eggs one at a time, blending well.
- Add vanilla and almond extracts.
- Add sour cream and blend well.
- Pour into crust.

- Bake for 60 - 70 minutes. Jiggle slightly - cake should not look liquid at all.
- Run knife around the outside edge but do not remove from pan.
- Cool on counter 10 - 15 minutes, then chill in refrigerator overnight or at least 4 hours.
- Drizzle with elderberry syrup and spoon mixed berries on top.

JUNE

June 20th

Dear Mama,

Remember how you used to turn our birthday celebrations into birth month celebrations? Every day of the month was marked with something special. Well, this month, even though it's not quite the same, I feel like I've awakened to something to celebrate almost every single day, reminding me so much of you!

The first day of June, we put a brand new refrigerator on a 30-day lay-away at Home Depot. It's a gorgeous bright white side-by-side unit I've drooled over since starting this project, but that we would never have been able to afford. One day, though, while we were there shopping for cupboard door hardware, Christian grabbed my arm and pointed. An orange-aproned man walked up to it with a folder full of fluorescent orange labels and slapped one on the front of it, marking it down almost half price. It was still more than we wanted to pay, but I could see Christian's mind spinning as quickly as mine was to try to reallocate funds from one place to another to make it happen. His eyebrows went up in question, I nodded, mentally kissing goodbye the new dishwasher I'd insisted I couldn't do without, and we practically tackled the poor guy on the spot.

You should have seen us, Mama. Even you might have been embarrassed.

No. I take that back. You would have started hollering at him to get his attention from across the store. Anyway, without explaining, Christian reached over and ripped that sale tag off the front of the fridge and I started talking about Divine timing and cottage industries and calling the poor man—his name was Alex—my own personal Hermes. He stood there agape, unable to decide whether we were excited or angry about the price drop, or just plain crazy, and clearly wondering if we meant to steal the thing right out from under his nose. He actually moved to stand in front of it as though to say, "Over my dead body."

Christian put a hand on my arm and I stopped talking long enough for him to explain to Alex that no, I hadn't mistaken him for someone else, that he was, in a sense, a messenger of good news to us, and that yes, we had every intention of buying it if there was a way we could put a deposit down now and hold it until we did a little shuffling of funds. Then he handed the tag back to the guy, who slapped it back in place on the freezer side of the appliance.

I could tell by the look in Alex' eyes that he still wasn't sure if he was safe, but he swallowed bravely, pulled out a black marker, and wrote SOLD across the tag, then turned and barked, "Follow me."

He led us to a manager station, explained the situation in low tones, leaning forward so we couldn't see his face (I'm pretty sure he rolled his eyes at least twice), and we put down our deposit and walked out of that store with a receipt and a 30-day layaway.

We forgot all about the cupboard door hardware and had to go back the next day, and I found a set of cut glass knobs that had one missing from the packet. Yep. Half price. Instead of eight, there were only seven, and we only need six, so I have an extra one I can mount on a pretty board and use as an apron hook.

The day before my birthday, we had dinner with Christian's folks. His big sister, Shannon, and her hubby, Truman, and their twin preteen boys were there, and we brought Dad along, too. Well, his whole family pitched in, dragging Dad in on it with them, and got me the French doors of my dreams! They love to do "Family Project" gifts, pooling their resources when there's something big on someone's wish list. I was so overwhelmed.

See, it was the first time we'd had a meal with everyone together since Julian. Since before I moved out. I knew Shannon had been really angry at me for running, and had even suggested Christian file for divorce. I know, though, that she doesn't hate me, Mama, but hated what I was doing to him. That night, after dinner, the guys headed off to the living room to watch a game, while Shannon, me, and Charlotte (Christian's mom) settled on stools at a counter in the kitchen, sipping coffee, and catching up.

For several minutes, we skirted the big issues and talked about the twins, about Charlotte's book club, and about my Elderberry Croft products and plans. Well, that segued rather conveniently into questions about the actual Elderberry Croft. Starting with Kathy, I regaled them with stories about my beloved neighbors, but halfway through telling them about Andrea and George's loss, Shannon abruptly stood up, pushed away from the counter, and circled around to the sink. I didn't say a word as she turned the water on, then off, then on full blast again. It was like she was trying to get her words to flow like the water, but couldn't find the on/off lever. Finally, she turned around, crossed her arms over her chest, leaned her hip against the sink, and faced me. Her eyes glistened, and a single tear tracked down each cheek from the corners of her eyes.

"Why? Why did you leave like that?" Her voice cracked and the rasp of it was more accusing than any words she could utter. "Do you think those people needed you more than Christian did?"

When I didn't respond right away, she continued. "He lost both of you, Willow." She swallowed, hard, and whispered, "How did you expect him to bear it?"

No one else had put it that way before, and suddenly, I was twelve again, and Daddy was sitting across from me at our little scarred oak table, telling me that you were coming home from the hospital, Mama. I couldn't understand why he was so sad—this was good news, right? His bloodshot eyes, the skin beneath them smudged with fatigue and despair, met mine. Two tears slid from the corners of his eyes, just like Shannon's.

"She's coming home to say goodbye," he'd said. "A nurse is coming, too, to help keep her comfortable." Then he dropped his head in his hands and began to weep.

I didn't know what to do, Mama. I was twelve. I told myself to get up and go to him, to put my arms around him and comfort him, but I couldn't move. I just sat across from him, watching his body shake. It was almost soundless at first, like he was trying to hold it all in, but when a sob tore out of him, I jumped, the sound startling me into motion. I leapt up out of my chair, toppling it over behind me, and fled the room. I ran and ran and ran, abandoning him to his grief, just like I did Christian. What is wrong with me, Mama?

It was almost as if I had convinced myself if I wasn't there when you came home, then you wouldn't be able to say goodbye to me. And if you couldn't say goodbye, then you wouldn't be able to die on us. I headed into the woods, along the trail that went past the heap of boulders—you know that one where the nettle comes back so heartily year after year—and on up to the ridge to that glorious stand of birch trees. I had a surprise planned for you in the circle of those trees. The whole time you were in the hospital, I'd spent almost every afternoon up there, turning that little hollow into a sanctuary for when you came home, on the mend. I was going to take you there, let you rest on a blanket on a pile of leaves, and read to you while you got your strength back. I'd even constructed a little shelter for you, in case the sun got too hot or the breeze too cold, a three-sided thing made from branches tied together with twine and braced against the thick trunk of an ancient tree long ago fallen and returned to the earth. In my shock-addled mind, I reasoned I'd wait for you there, for surely, if you came to me there, it meant you were getting better, and would not die.

Daddy. Poor Daddy. He searched high and low for me. I could hear him every once in a while, being up higher than he, his voice winding its way along the trail to me. I curled up inside the little fort, hands over my ears, and promptly fell asleep.

I awoke to darkness all around me, and in a panic, stood up without thinking, knocking over the fort, and making such a ruckus, every wild animal that hadn't known I was there before, surely did then. Terror gripped me and I started screaming like a wild animal myself, and suddenly, Daddy was there, that headlamp flashlight he loves to wear shining in my eyes, his arms around me. I could hear other voices in the darkness, too, and I recognized many of them; friends and neighbors come to help look for me.

Shannon's words reminded me of Daddy's that night. "Would you have me lose both of you at the same time? I couldn't bear it, Willow."

I think that's why I ran, I suppose, after Julian died. Maybe part of me, that twelve-year-old girl part of me, thought if I didn't have to look at his empty crib or listen to the stillness of the house around me anymore, then maybe he wasn't really gone.

I tried to explain the best I could to these other two important women in my husband's life, but my words sounded empty and selfish to my ears. I finally stopped talking and just stared down into my half-full cup of coffee.

Charlotte stepped in then, drawing Shannon close to her side, and reached out to press a cool palm to my cheek. "I'm truly glad you're home, Willow, and I love you as though you were my own daughter. But no more running, you hear? We are your family and we are a safe place to hide when you need sanctuary." She turned to Shannon, and I could see her squeeze her daughter's shoulder. "Right, Shan?"

A moment's hesitation, then Shannon reached for my hand and held it between both of her own. "Run *to* us, Willow, not from us, okay?"

They were both very pushy about it, Mama, and something shifted and opened up to them, a place inside of me I'd thought only belonged to you. Family. It's good to really belong. A truly wonderful birthday gift.

And speaking of belonging, and family, and of Andrea and George, on the 10th, Christian and I attended their small family wedding at her parents' house. They have a lovely, huge backyard, and even though it was really hot during the day, once the sun started going down, the breeze picked up and cooled things nicely. The wedding wasn't until five o'clock, followed by a delicious meal catered by a local Mexican restaurant; George's choice.

Then on the 16th, Myra and Jackson tied the knot, too! They did so at the courthouse, but they followed up with a potluck out at The Coach House, and we went to that, too. There's another new tenant in Elderberry Croft—the second one since I moved out—but no one knows anything about him and he wasn't at the potluck. Maybe he'll attend the 4th of July barbecue next month. I got a secret thrill, though, to hear everyone still referring to the little cottage as "Willow's Place," or even "Elderberry Croft," and not just "Space #12."

Yes, I brought a basket full of pastries. The favorite was my scones, but I think it was the maple cream cheese frosting more than anything. People love that stuff.

And now, here it is the 20th, and the fridge is being delivered today sometime, then the French doors will be installed tomorrow.

Poor Princess Baggy. She'll be locked out of the kitchen for good once those go up. By the way, she's claimed your old bathrobe as hers. I left it on the floor one morning—I'd used it because mine was in the wash—and I discovered her burrowed down into it three different times that day. I moved it to the living room to see what she'd do. Sure enough, the next morning, I found her curled up in a little ball inside the folds of it, only her little black nose sticking out of it. Christian is happy about that. He always said it was little weird to see me in my mother's bathrobe, that he didn't know whether to kiss me, or cover his eyes. So I bought myself a new one for my birthday, a thick, smoky blue thing that feels like I'm wearing a cloud. Christian says I do look like an angel in it, so maybe the whole cloud thing has bearing.

Life is good, Mama. Even the hard stuff, like talking to Christian's women, is good in the end. Worth getting up each day for. Worth taking another breath for.

I miss you. Will you do me a favor? Will you squeeze Julian so tightly for me that he cries, then cuddle with him and kiss him and make him feel better and tell him I love him?

No, never mind. That sounds psycho. Squeeze him so tightly he laughs, then cuddle with him and kiss him and just tell him I love him, okay?

Willow's Elderberry Scones

Ingredients
2 Cups All-Purpose Flour
½ Cup Sugar
1 Teaspoon Baking Powder
¼ Teaspoon Baking Soda
½ Teaspoon Salt
8 Tablespoons Frozen Unsalted Butter
½ Cup Elderberries (fresh, frozen, or dried)
½ Cup Sour Cream
1 Large Egg
1 Teaspoon of Sugar and Cinnamon

Cooking Instructions:
- Adjust oven rack to lower-middle position and preheat oven to 400 degrees.
- In a medium bowl, mix dry ingredients.
- Grate frozen butter into the flour mixture (use large holes on grater).Use fingers to work butter into flour mixture until it resembles coarse meal.
- Stir in elderberries.
- In a small bowl, whisk sour cream and egg until smooth.
- Using a fork, stir sour cream mixture into flour mixture until large dough clumps form.
- Use your hands to press the dough against the bowl into a ball. (The dough may seem too sticky, but it will come together.)Place on a lightly floured surface and pat into a 7- to 8-inch circle about 3/4-inch thick.
- Sprinkle with sugar and cinnamon.
- Use a sharp knife to cut into 8 triangles; place on a cookie sheet (preferably lined with parchment paper), about 1

inch apart.
- Bake until golden, about 15 to 17 minutes.
- Cool for 5 minutes and serve warm or at room temperature.

Maple Cream Cheese Frosting
16 Ounces Softened Cream Cheese (not whipped)
½ Cup Softened Butter
4 Cups Powdered Sugar
¼ Cup Maple Syrup (Use the real deal if you have it. If not, the maple flavored syrup will work in a pinch.)

Instructions
- Beat cream cheese and butter in large bowl until well combined.
- Add sugar and maple syrup and stir until smooth. Store in refrigerator until needed.

Options
Cranberry-Orange Scones
Add a generous teaspoon of finely grated orange rind (zest) to the dry ingredients and substitute dried cranberries for the elderberries.

Lemon-Blueberry Scones
Add a generous teaspoon of finely grated lemon rind (zest) to the dry ingredients and substitute dried blueberries for the elderberries.

Cherry-Almond Scones
Add 1/2 tsp. almond extract to the sour cream mixture and substitute dried cherries for the elderberries.

JULY

July 10th

Dear Mama,

Last week we went to The Coach House again to celebrate the 4th of July with the gang. We had several options for the day—Christian's folks invited us to go to the park with them and their church group, Shannon and her guys went to a pool party at a friend's and asked us to join them. Even Daddy called to see if we had plans and said we could go hang out and watch the fireworks from the back lawn of the retirement home with him and all his girlfriends. But during Myra and Jackson's wedding potluck last month, we'd all agreed that we wanted to do another barbecue and contraband firework show again this year, so that's what we did.

It was wonderful, Mama, in so many ways, but so different. I couldn't help but think of Thomas Wolfe and his George Weber character in "You can't go home again." Of course, there's nothing threatening about my visits to the trailer park, but like George, I experience a sense of having been displaced, even if by my own hand, and left floundering a bit. It's not just Elderberry Croft, either. I still feel that way a little about coming back here, to the home Christian and I have. I *am* home, but it's not the same, and not just because of Julian's absence. We are the same people, Christian and I, but we're changed in ways that are almost too small to be able to put a finger on, yet significant enough to create ripples in what I once had thought was eternal and immovable between us.

The guy living in Elderberry Croft now is the second tenant to stay there since I moved out. He's a long distance truck driver, like Carney (purely coincidental—they don't know each other), and he's on the road two or three weeks at a time, then home for several days, before he's off and driving again. He was on a road trip last week, so I still haven't met him. Kathy says he's a nice enough man. That means he's acknowledged her dogs and her, in that order, at least once since moving in. But the little cottage seems to be fading somehow, and it makes me sad to see it so... utilitarian. It's beginning to feel more like just plain old Space #12. Sigh.

Kathy and Myra also told me what little they knew about the woman who'd first moved into Elderberry Croft (I refuse to stop calling it that, no matter how it feels) the month after I left. Marital problems, presumably. She came with the bare minimum, stayed less than three months, and left the place looking as though she'd never been. Nora. Her name was Nora. They said the woman kept to herself the whole time she was here. "Not like you," Kathy said, rolling her eyes at me. "You wouldn't mind your own business, and forced yourself on everyone." Whatever her reasons for being there, I hope Nora found what she was looking for while she was tucked into the arms of Elderberry Croft.

Almost everyone came to the potluck, even Andrea and

Elderberry Days — BECKY DOUGHTY

George! Andrea pulled me aside, so reminiscent of last year, and told me they were going to try to get pregnant again. I hugged her hard before she could ask about us. I saw the question in her eyes, but I don't know how to answer that. Christian and I are in such a strange place right now. In some ways, it's like we're newlyweds all over again, figuring out what it means for two to become one once more. I don't know that we're ready to try to figure out what it means for two to become three again. Not yet.

There's a new guy, Mitch, living in the upstairs apartment where Andrea and George were. He's a friend of Jackson's and has settled in well at the park, hanging out on Myra's front porch playing cards with the rest of the guys. He looks like he's in his late sixties or early seventies, and he's kinda quiet, but from what I gathered, his wife recently passed away. I'm glad he's at The Coach House where there are so many people who can understand.

Pru and Carney came to the potluck this year. They're in the throes of packing up Pru's apartment in the main Coach House. They got married right before Carney had his heart surgery last year. She insisted they do it before because she wanted the authority, as his wife, to make certain he got the best treatment possible during his hospital stay and recovery. They're so cute together, Mama. Anyway, now that he's been given a clean bill of health, they're going to get a place together. Carney says it's the bathroom. "It was cute when it was just Pru, but there's something wrong with a guy like me standing on a pink fur rug and drying off with leopard print towels." I have to admit, although the visual was more than I needed, I agree whole-heartedly. As much of a big bear as Carney is, I never could juxtapose him over the whole wild kingdom theme Pru has going. I wonder what their house is going to look like—I heard Pru talking to Vivien about carnivals and Coney Island, and I can see it. They remind me a little of a circus strong man and his fancy lady, but I would never say so, just because it seems so cliché and those two are anything but cliché.

Eddie and Shelly are still an item, but I think they're perfectly content with the way things are, having their own places right across the footbridge from each other. It's a little strange to me because I'm not in either of their shoes, but I really think they like being able to go home to their own places at the end of the night. Even with all the tenants moving in and out of the place, real change comes carefully, if not slowly, at The Coach House, I'm telling you, especially with someone like Shelly. Which is why Eddie is good for her. He's there, he's not going anywhere, and she can blossom at her own pace. They seem very happy with each other, and she's come out of her shell so much since I first met her. Eddie is solid, and responsible, and predictable, and Shelly thinks he's the cat's meow. Which is saying a lot, coming from the resident Cat Lady.

Myra and Jackson. They've been married a month now. Myra refused to move out of her darling little trailer, so Jackson moved in with her. I was afraid Al was going to be jealous, but he seems to have taken this all in stride. He's an interesting guy, Mama, but I just can't read him well enough to feel totally at ease around him. Out of necessity and self-preservation, he's always kept things pretty close to the vest, and I suppose ingrained habits like that are hard to break. But even now, with everyone knowing about his poor wife, her passing, and his part in it, he still seems wary and watchful to me. Not like he's going to hurt anyone, but like he's afraid someone might think he would. I do pray a nice woman comes along who can break down that wall and help release him from the prison he's lived in for so long. I don't know if he's a believer or not, but I do know Christian prayed often with him while he was helping Al sort out all the fallout from his wife's death. I just can't imagine it's healthy for the heart to live every day, looking over your shoulder like that, though, Mama. He still seems stuck to me. He looks good, though. He's lost a few pounds, Myra says he hardly drinks at all anymore (she would know, little Mother Hen that she is), so that's all good.

Speaking of drinking, Donny stopped in for a while, which surprised me, considering what a disaster last year's July 4th celebration was for him. He did bring a woman named Shawna with him, so that eased my mind. Christian's, too. Even though he'd never met the infamous Banks brother, Donny and Eddie look enough alike that there's no mistaking they're family. And Donny did make a point to give me the once over quite openly until Christian stepped up behind me, one arm going around my waist to pull me back against him (a little more aggressively than necessary, I thought), the other thrust out toward Donny as he introduced himself as "Christian. Willow's husband." It was as close to a "staking my claim" move as he's made on me since before we were married, and I have to tell you, Mama, I was suddenly extremely aware of how delicious a man "Willow's husband" is. I happily leaned back into him, not so much to ensure Donny got the message, but to let Christian know I was really quite thrilled to be claimed so boldly by him. Then Doc clapped an arm around Donny's shoulder and said something low and clipped in his ear. Donny's eyes got really big for just a moment before the two of them wandered off to talk to Eddie. I have no idea what that conversation covered, but I don't think Donny even so much as looked at me the rest of the time they were there.

Shawna seemed nice enough, but I have to tell you, Mama, it was like sitting next to a porcupine with her quills slicked back. She spent most of her time watching Donny, almost like a parole officer... or a babysitter. When she wasn't watching him, she was sizing up us women, even though we were all there with our husbands or boyfriends. As uncomfortable as that made everyone, I couldn't help but feel sorry for her. I heard the talk swirling around in her wake. I guess she's been through several break-ups and reunions with Donny over the years, and most of them have been because of his drug and alcohol abuse, which apparently translates into domestic abuse in his case. She's one of the walking wounded.

According to Edith, Donny's mom, he's been sober for a whole year now, but I'm not so sure. I have very little experience with alcoholics or addicts, but his behavior seemed kinda shady to me. Furtive. That's a good word for the way he was acting. He kept disappearing, sometimes alone, sometimes with Shawna, and I think (don't quote me on this) that Shawna had something pretty potent in her water bottle, one of those huge, hot pink 64-ounce sports bottles with the foam grip and the accordion plastic straw. Doc made some comment about her not getting too close to the barbecue at one point, lest we have fireworks a little early. She and Donny left shortly after that, but I overheard Pru mention to Eddie that Shawna had asked her a lot of questions about her apartment. I can't imagine Eddie being okay with Donny moving into the park on a more permanent and official basis, with or without Shawna, but what's that saying? Keep your friends close and your enemies closer? I don't think Donny is an enemy, per se, but he's definitely on shaky footing with pretty much everyone there. Except Edith. I'm sure that's why Edith was making such a point about him being sober, though. I know she'd like to have him close, but at least she has put her foot down about him moving in with her again, even temporarily. Or maybe Eddie put his foot down about it. Goodness. The mess we can make of life when we live only for ourselves.

I'm sad for Donny, that with so many people rooting for him, with the extent his family and friends have gone to help him, that he's missing out on being the man he could be by trying to stay the child he no longer is. I'm sad for Shawna in ways I can't even begin to put to words. I'm sad for Edith, who clearly struggles with accepting the truth of Donny's condition, not because she can't see it, but because she loves him so much and hope allows her to keep her blinders on. I'm sad for Eddie, too. He seems to handle it well, Mama, but every once in a while, I see him look at Edith, waiting... for what? Approval, I'm certain. She misses all the things he does for her, all he does for the people who live at the park, for the place itself, because she's so focused on what little Donny does.

So yes, the day was bittersweet for me. So many things have changed and moved forward, progressed, since this time last year. Andrea and George, married and thinking about a new baby, Joe and Vivien gone public with their marriage, Myra and Jackson, Carney and Pru, Eddie and Shelley. But Elderberry Croft, Al, Donny. Even Doc, there alone. His youngest daughter, Janeen, stops by periodically to check on her dad and they seem to have the makings of a fairly healthy relationship in the works, but he's heard nothing from Tracy, his older girl. He still hasn't seen his wife, but he did receive a letter from Eleanor telling him she's proud of him for taking the steps he is. She's not ready to see him again, but is willing to communicate through letters for now.

"For how long?" I asked. Doc just shrugged and said it was up to Eleanor. Sometimes cycles are too ingrained in us. Even when those extra pushes come, and opportunities arise for new beginnings, for second and third and fourth chances, and change pries its way into every nook and cranny, even then, we dig in our heels and try to force things to stay the same, panicking when they charge ahead without our permission. But the thing is, change is actually what brings us full circle in the end, right? And to deny it is to deny life, to deny God and His plan for our lives.

Listen to this, Mama. This is what I love about Wolfe; how he captures this struggle so well.

"Child, child, have patience and belief, for life is many days, and each present hour will pass away. Son, son, you have been mad and drunken, furious and wild, filled with hatred and despair, and all the dark confusions of the soul—but so have we. You found the earth too great for your one life, you found your brain and sinew smaller than the hunger and desire that fed on them—but it has been this way with all men. You have stumbled on in darkness, you have been pulled in opposite directions, you have faltered, you have missed the way, but, child, this is the chronicle of the earth."

Isn't that the saddest thing you've ever read? Do all people walk through murky places like this? Is that why his description of despair resonates so deeply with us? Or is it just me?

And yet, he then offers hope to those who have walked

those endless dark paths. What a wonderful word. Hope.

"And now, because you have known madness and despair, and because you will grow desperate again before you come to evening, we who have stormed the ramparts of the furious earth and been hurled back, we who have been maddened by the unknowable and bitter mystery of love, we who have hungered after fame and savored all of life, the tumult, pain, and frenzy, and now sit quietly by our windows watching all that henceforth never more shall touch us—we call upon you to take heart, for we can swear to you that these things pass."

As gut-wrenchingly beautiful as Wolfe's words are, they are a mere echo of God promises, aren't they?

Hope. I cling to that hope. Every day, I grab on with both hands and hold on tight. The journey out of despair isn't easy. In fact, it's often arduous and even treacherous at times. But I refuse to lie down and be overwhelmed. I am learning to embrace change, to take another step. Then another.

I took Daddy some of my elderberry banana bread yesterday. I tried out a new recipe and he's always game to be my guinea pig. He gave it three thumbs up: two of his own and one from Glinda, the little lady from housekeeping who came by while we were visiting. He gave her the rest of it to take home to her family. She speaks very little English, but she and Daddy do a lot of thumbs upping and thumbs downing to communicate. Anyway, we talked for a long time about what it means to choose to live after facing death; yours, Julian's, even Daddy's friends. He says rarely a month goes by that there isn't another goodbye party at Fairhaven. They have goodbye parties whenever anyone dies, but Daddy isn't sure whether it's to honor the person who died, or to celebrate the fact that the party-goers are still alive, I think. Anyway, did you know that one of Daddy's favorite quotes is from *You Can't Go Home Again*? "This is man, who, if he can remember ten golden moments of joy and happiness out of all his years, ten moments unmarked by care, unseamed by aches or itches, has power to lift himself with his expiring breath and say: "I have lived upon this earth and known glory!" He says he wants that last line, "I have lived upon this earth and known glory!" on his tombstone.

In bed last night, as we lay curled together in the dark, I asked Christian if he had a favorite line from the book. I thought it might be "The guilty fleeth where no man pursueth," something he's quoted many a times because of his career choice. But my heart still hurts today remembering his sleep-lulled voice rumbling against my cheek pressed to his back. "It seems to me that in the orbit of our world, you are the North Pole, I the South—so much in balance, in agreement—and yet... the whole world lies between."

He woke me up before going to work this morning, however, bringing me a cup of coffee to aid in prying open my eyes. He sat on the edge of the bed and held my hand, toying with my wedding ring for several minutes while I put away my dreams and accepted the new day's existence. He didn't apologize, but I heard the regret in his voice. He must have felt my hot tears after I was sure he'd fallen asleep.

"Last night I told you one of my favorite quotes from *You Can't Go Home Again*," he said, ever so gently. "And it is one of my favorites, because I have felt the truth of those words resonate in the marrow of my bones from the moment I first met you until this one. And I know I'll feel the truth of those words until the day I die. Willow, I *want* to spend every moment of this life crossing worlds to reach you. You are my grandest adventure, my life's journey, my heart's pursuit."

I couldn't speak. It was almost too much for me to bear so early in the morning, but I sat still as a stone and let his verbal caress wash over me. He brushed his fingertips along one of my cheekbones, smoothing back the Medusa hair from my face.

"But this morning, when I got out of bed, you reached for my pillow and smiled in your sleep, and another line came to me. I looked it up because I wanted to get it right."

He laid his long-fingered hand on top of my head, and leaned forward to kiss my brow. Then, like a blessing, he quoted, "Peace fell upon her spirit. Strong comfort and assurance bathed her whole being. Life was so solid and splendid, and so good."

Maybe Thomas Wolfe is wrong after all, Mama. I have come home, and it is so good.

Willow's Banana Elderberry Bread

Dry Ingredients
2 Cups Whole Wheat Flour
2 Cups White Flour
½ Cup White Sugar
½ Cup Brown Sugar
1 Teaspoon Salt
5 Teaspoons Baking Powder
1 Teaspoon Baking Soda

Wet Ingredients
½ Cup Canola Oil
2 Large Eggs
1 Cup Milk
½ Cup Sour Cream
1 Teaspoon Vanilla
2 Cups Mashed Bananas (about 5)
½ Cup Fresh Elderberries (or reconstituted elderberries)
1 Cup of Chopped Nuts (optional)

Cooking Instructions:
- Combine all of the dry ingredients. Set aside.
- Blend all of the wet ingredients with the bananas.
- Mix dry ingredients into wet, but do not over mix. Batter will be lumpy.
- Stir in elderberries and/or nuts.
- Divide into two 9x5-inch greased loaf pans.
- Bake at 350 degrees for 50-60 minutes, or until toothpick inserted in center comes out clean. Do not overcook.
- Cool on racks for about ten minutes before cutting.
- Best eaten warm and slathered in butter.

AUGUST

August 8th

Oh Mama,

Yesterday, I got a call from Myra. Al died in his sleep a few nights ago. Myra and Jackson go with Al to Peggy's Diner every Tuesday morning (I hear Peggy's has the best biscuits and gravy ever, but no one does them better than Daddy, right?). So when Al didn't show, then didn't answer the phone, they walked over to his place to collect him, assuming he'd just gotten hung up chatting with Eddie or another neighbor.

When they couldn't locate him, Jackson looked in the bedroom window—I guess the blinds were up enough to see inside—and there he was, still in bed, looking for all the world like he'd simply slept in. Jackson called 911 and Myra ran for Eddie. According to the medical report, it was a heart attack, but he apparently went quickly and peacefully, because the bedclothes were hardly disturbed around him.

There's no funeral, mainly because there's no family to see to it. Actually, there is a sister, Christian told me, but she and Al have been estranged for years and when she was contacted (I wonder who did that? The coroner? The hospital? Or did poor Eddie have to contact her?), she simply said she was sorry to hear it and would stake no claims on him or his property.

So, we're having another potluck out at the trailer park next week; a goodbye party this time.

I don't know if I can stand it, Mama. When I told Christian last night, he actually teared up, which made me cry again, too. We talked late into the night, feet touching and fingers laced together, the August heat pressing up against the windows but unable to breech the cocoon of our air-conditioned comfort. Tucked into each other, our bedroom is a sanctuary from the suffering of the world outside our door. I couldn't help but think of Al, lying there alone in the dark, his own heart attacking him while at his most vulnerable. Even if he could have called out for help, there was no one there to hear him. There hasn't been anyone to hear him cry out in the night for most of his life, Mama. It just breaks my heart.

Why did he have to die now? Now! Now, when he was finally freed up from the prison he'd spent his whole life in, finally free to live again? Was his life wasted? The sacrifices he made to keep his Maggie cared for, knowing she could never care for him the same way, and maybe never had. I can't stop thinking maybe God might have gotten this one wrong.

I know, I know. Greater love hath no man than he lay down his life for his friend. Straight out of the Bible. And Al, of all people, has laid down his life for Maggie. But I've read that passage in John 15, Mama, and there's more to it than that. In verse 11, it says, "These things I have spoken to you so that My joy may be in you, and that your joy may be full."

Was Al's joy full? Did the sacrifice of his love give him a fullness of joy? It goes on to say that we are chosen so that we would bear fruit. What kind of fruit did Al bear? Was it Maggie's right to take, and take some more, and even more, from Al practically up until the moment he died?

For better or for worse. Clearly Al meant that, Mama. Because he stayed for worse, and worse, and even worse.

And maybe that's why I'm angry. I'm ashamed all over again. Al stayed and stayed and stayed; through every test and trial, his love for and commitment to Maggie stayed true.

At the moment *my* love was tested, I ran.

~ ~ ~

August 14th

I'm sitting in the kitchen at my little work table, staring at the rows and rows of elderberry preserves and jam I've canned over the last couple of weeks for when I get the stamp of approval from Public Health Department. I've been holding my pen over this blank page for almost an hour now, unable to put into words what is on my heart, but feeling I must. Princess Baggy is pacing just on the other side of the French doors, glowering at me, plotting my demise, I'm certain, because I won't let her in. Christian is avoiding me completely, and for good reason. I feel like a live wire, ready to spark and flare at him if he gets too close. Anger makes my synapses misfire, and I can't find the words I need. I do my best gardening when I'm like this, but it's brutally hot outside and I'm already feeling drained from the day.

This morning was the goodbye party for Al out at The Coach House. We gathered out in the back field opposite

Joe's place. There are a few trees over there, and both Joe and Eddie dragged their grills out under them, but by noon, we were all wilting in the heat. We ended up heading over to Pru's place to eat and talk about Al. Her living room is good sized, and air conditioned, so we brought all the food in there to keep everyone from getting food poisoning. Her little yard is in full shade and butts right up to the stream, like Elderberry Croft, so we all took shoes off and sat with our feet in the water or wandered in and out of the apartment. Pru and Carney found a place they both like and will be out the end of this month, so the apartment was nearly empty already, which created plenty of room for people to mill about in the cool air.

Fruit. Mama, Al bore fruit after all. And today, I got a taste of it. Every single person at the park had something to share about Al, about something he'd done for them. Even the new guy in Elderberry Croft, Bill Jensen. Bill showed up in blue jeans rolled at the cuff and an almost white shirt, his hair pomaded into an Elvis coif. He can't be much younger than fifty, and I can't tell if he's stylin' with his rockabilly look, or if he's never changed his style in fifty years. Regardless, he was very sweet about Al helping him change his tire the week after he moved in. Todd Adams, the young kid upstairs from Pru and Carney, paid his respects, too, although I think he was all about the free all-you-can-eat buffet potluck more than anything. He didn't hang around long after his third plateful. Anyway, I guess Al had seen him struggling up the stairs with what little furniture he had, and offered to help. Todd worried that he might have contributed to Al's heart attack, "Making him strain like that, and all," but everyone assured him that no one held him in any way responsible.

Kathy said Al always put down a bowl of milk for her cat, Lucy, who visited him every day. Edith said she always felt safe knowing Al was right next door, keeping an eye on the comings and goings of the park, and that she hadn't slept well since he'd passed, leaving his place empty. Al apparently had a bread machine, and baked bread for Richard and Patti once a week. Eddie said Al was as dependable as clockwork. "He paid his space rent on time every month, and not once in the years I've been here, have I ever had to ask him to tidy things up around his place. He was steady as a rock, a man to depend on, come hell or high water." Shelly said he always took the time to poke his head out and wave at her as she drove by on Friday mornings. "Like clockwork," she said, echoing Eddie. "He was part of my Friday routine and I'm going to miss him terribly." Coming from anyone else, that might have sounded odd, but for Shelly, changing her routine is tragic. She truly will miss him terribly.

Joe and Vivien couldn't be there, but they sent a beautiful plant in Al's name. Everyone agreed that Myra and Jackson would take it home with them. Myra started out by saying she trusted Al to water her patio plants (and she has lots of them) any time she was gone, then she began to cry so hard no one could understand the rest of what she said. I'm pretty sure it was something about him being the brother she never had (although I kinda thought that was what Jackson was until they got married), how he loved her cooking, and always told her how pretty she was. Jackson only said that Al was a good man, the best of men, and his place across the game table would stay empty in his honor.

Christian talked briefly about his time spent with Al. No one had mentioned Al's Maggie up to that point, so he did.

He didn't break any oaths or confidentiality laws, but spoke, almost on behalf of her, I suppose. He'd talked to the hospital staff where she'd lived, and shared some of the things they said about Al; his faithfulness, his commitment, his sacrificial love for his wife. "Like you said, Eddie. Steady as a rock, a man to depend on. I know Maggie would say the same thing."

Doc. Well, Doc said more than everyone else put together ... without uttering a word. He stood, cleared his throat twice, swallowed hard a few times, then shook his head, raised his flask, saluted, and sat down again. They used to sit together on Al's porch, or on Myra's, Mama, not saying a word to each other. I think words might have robbed the pure eloquence of Doc's silent farewell. We all took a sip of whatever was in front of us in acknowledgment of that friendship.

Al's fruit. Like a cluster of elderberries. One tiny little berry may seem insignificant, but when you bring them all together like that? *Not* wasted, Mama. Not wasted at all. Broken, perhaps, but unwilling to let it defeat him. Instead, he did what he could in the tiny circle in which he lived. He bloomed where he planted. Like my little elderberry tree at Elderberry Croft.

So why am I angry at Christian?

On the drive home, I started to tell him how sorry I was for running, how Al had been such a better person than I was, staying the course, standing firm, steady as a rock, and how could Christian ever trust me— He freaked out on me, Mama.

F.R.E.A.K.E.D. O.U.T.

Basically, he said I was being selfish and that it was time to get over myself. Get over myself? Get *over* myself? My scalp is tingling right now—my hair must be standing on end—and if I wasn't sweating from the heat outside, I'd be sweating from the boiling blood in my veins. He said it was time to stop wearing my guilt and shame like a *cilice*, pulling it out whenever I started to get too happy and content with things.

I tried to explain about the broken pieces of my life, that I didn't know how to be whole again, because I didn't even know where all the pieces were anymore.

He said I sounded like a walking cliché.

Then I freaked out.

F.R.E.A.K.E.D. O.U.T.

I asked him to explain to me *how* he could just get up and get on with life after killing our son.

Yep. I said that.

I'm not angry at Christian, Mama. I'm angry at me.

He's right. Once again, he's right. I'm a walking tragedy, and you know what? I'm *sick* of it. I'm sick of feeling all fragile and crumbly on the inside and raw and exposed on the outside. I'm sick of not feeling whole. I'm sick of this horrific hair shirt I've condemned myself to wear. And of the one I think Christian should be wearing, too.

(I had to look it up. How does he know these things? A *cilice* is one of those coarse hair shirts worn under clothing to induce discomfort and/or pain as an act of penance, contrition, or mourning, etc. Mine is a humdinger—now *that's* the kind of word I like—but apparently, the one I designed for Christian is made of fiberglass and steel wool.)

He's right. It's time. I'm going to gather what pieces I already have and give them to God. Let *Him* use them for whatever He thinks He can make of them, of me.

I'm going to take the fire in my belly right now and use it to burn our *cilices* to ashes.

And I'm going to go apologize one more time to my husband, demand he forgives me for being selfish and afraid, fragile when I *know* I'm not. You always taught me that, Mama. Life is to be handled with care, but God did not make us fragile. That's fear. "For God has not given us a spirit of fear and timidity, but of power, love, and self-discipline." That's straight out of the Bible, too, and I'm claiming it. I want to live a life of power and love and self-discipline, the kind that comes from God, not me.

I just heard the front door open and close and now there are footsteps coming my way. It's uncanny how he seems to know when I need him.

Now he's standing outside the French doors beside Princess Baggy. He has a scraggly bouquet of flowers in his hand—what little he could find from my wilting garden, I believe.

He's not wearing any shirt—hair or otherwise. I know it's probably because it's really hot outside, but now it's starting to get hot inside.

I'm blushing and grinning like a besotted idiot.

I love that man.

I've got to go, Mama.

Willow's Elderberry Preserves

Elderberry Preserves Ingredients
4 or 5 8-oz Jars and 2-Piece Canning Lids
4 Cups Mashed Elderberries (about 4 ½ cups fresh berries)
¼ Cup Lemon Juice
1 Packet of Pectin (Sure-Jell)
1 Cup Honey (room temperature)
1 Teaspoon Almond Extract

Preserves Jar Preparation
Prepare your jars and lids ahead of time. Wash jars, screw bands, and flat lid tops in hot, soapy water. Rinse carefully. Place jars on clean cookie sheet in a 250 degree oven until ready to use, and place lids in a clean bowl or pot. Bring a few quarts of water to a boil. Pour boiling water over lids, and leave them to sit in the water until needed.

Cooking Instructions
- In a heavy-bottomed sauce pan, combine elderberries and lemon juice.
- In a bowl, combine honey and pectin powder and mix well.
- Bring fruit mixture to a boil, then add honey mixture.
- Stir vigorously for 2-3 minutes, return mixture to a boil, then remove from heat.
- Add almond extract and mix well.
- Ladle preserves into jars, filling within 1/4 inch of the top, wipe rims clean, and close with lid and ring.
- Process in a boiling water bath for 5 minutes (add 1 minute for every 1000' feet above sea level).
- Preserves will set as they cool (allow at least 5-6 hours).

SEPTEMBER

September 25th

Dear Mama,

I've been meaning to write to you all month, but life keeps getting in the way. My kitchen is finished and I have an inspection scheduled with the Department of Public Health tomorrow, so it's been crazy town around here trying to get everything up to code. I'm confident we'll pass, but I still have butterflies in my stomach. Once we get that license, there will be no more excuses. Mama Dosh is chomping at the bit; she wants to do a major Holiday marketing deal to promote my stuff and some new holiday coffees she has. This has all taken so much longer than I could ever have imagined, but I know the time we've spent on this, the time we've spent working together toward our future, Christian and me, has been necessary for our healing.

Healing. It's been such a time of healing. You know how it is when you start making dinner and it's still light outside, but as you work, the sun goes down, and the room gets darker and darker without you even realizing it? Then someone walks in, flips on the light, and suddenly, you can see again, and it's rather startling. You thought you were just fine working in the shadows, squinting against the fading light.... That was me, Mama. I thought I was doing just fine, going about living my life back home again, content to make dinner in the dark. Then Christian walked in, turned on the light (by telling me to get rid of my hair shirt), and I could see in stark relief how difficult I was making things for both of us.

Anyway, we're doing well. The 2nd was our anniversary and I got up before Christian, made coffee for him for a change, opened a brand new jar of my elderberry preserves, and whipped up some yummy crepes for our breakfast. After we'd eaten I handed him his gift. "Happy Anniversary," I said, suddenly worried that he might think it unimaginative or too cliché. "For your office. Or wherever," I stammered, wrapping my hands around my empty coffee cup. He opened it carefully and smiled, his eyes shining in the morning sunlight. On one side of the two-paneled frame was a photo, taken by Daddy, of the three of us out on the lawn at the retirement home. It was Father's Day. Christian was crouched down, Julian sprawled across his bent knees, laughing and sun-drunk, me leaning over Christian's shoulder, reaching down to tickle Julian's exposed belly. It's the kind of picture that comes in a brand new frame, those staged snapshots of models pretending to be in love... but everything about the picture of us was real. On the other side was one of Christian's favorite photos of me, standing between the two elderberry trees he gave me for Valentine's Day. Dressed in his flannel shirt, my hair piled on top of my head in a wild mess, my dirty gardening gloves in one hand, the other holding a small umbel of elder flowers, I smiled at him with unfiltered joy.

"This is perfect, Willow. It's exactly what I wanted, what I needed from you." He touched my cheek in the picture. "You are so beautiful to me." Then he leaned forward and kissed my mouth. "Your gift is coming tonight." He left for work then, and I headed back to the kitchen, both of us looking forward to the evening we had planned.

We splurged and went out to dinner. A couple years ago we discovered this little Japanese restaurant that we absolutely love. It's family owned and operated and they greet us like old friends every time we come in. They were very happy to see us; we hadn't been in a long time. Christian explained to them about losing Julian when he made the reservation, and they were gracious and sensitive and honored that we were there to celebrate our anniversary in their establishment. I know those awkward moments are now permanently a part of our lives—people who don't know who ask questions that cut to the quick unintentionally—but we felt it best to tell them up front to make it easier for everyone.

The restaurant is part of a strip mall and looks like nothing special from the outside, and if you blink when driving by, you'd miss it altogether. But inside, it's all decorated in black lacquer and this deep green upholstery. There's a huge water feature in the corner with real water lilies and brightly-colored koi swimming around in it, fantastic artwork on sunset-colored walls, and the ceiling is festooned with twinkle lights and paper lanterns. It's like stepping into another world and we tend to act a little giddy whenever we go.

It was good timing. We needed to get out of here. Our every waking moment (at least mine, and much of my sleeping ones) have been focused on this kitchen and perfecting my recipes. If I'd had my way, I might have even called for an indefinite rain check. But Christian insisted, not just on going out, but on going out in style. So I made an appointment with Pru to have my hair trimmed, washed and styled. And then I came home and fixed it. *Don't* tell her, Mama, please. I looked like a red-headed Dolly Parton... well, *sans* "the girls." Nothing wrong with looking like Dolly Parton if you're Dolly Parton. Dolly Parton I am not. Willow suits me just fine, both in name and stature.

But I digress. So I left my hair down and loose, the way Christian likes it, and wore my favorite fancy dress, a blue flowy thing the color of a summer midnight sky. I have this shimmery charcoal bolero that goes perfectly with the dress. I haven't dressed up for a date in so long—not since I had Christian over for dinner at Elderberry Croft last December!—so I made Christian get ready in the guest bathroom while I got all gussied up in our room. Talk about butterflies! But it was worth it seeing the look in his eyes when I came down the hall toward him. Why does that man love me so much?

The weather was perfect, in spite of the September heat wave we always get here in Southern California. It had been in the upper 90s for weeks, not dropping below 75 degrees at night, but on the 2nd, it was actually in the mid-70s when we headed out, and there was a very slight breeze, just enough to clear the summer fug from the sky so we could see stars popping out on our way home. So romantic.

But even more romantic was the gift I received from Christian. I'm looking at it right now, and I still marvel at his ability to read me so well, to know instinctively how to speak to my heart. I know he sometimes feels like "the whole world lies between" us, but our hearts, our spirits, our souls are "in balance, in agreement" and I thank God for the gift of my husband every day.

When dinner was over, Yujiro and his wife, Amaya (her name means "night rain"—isn't that glorious?), surprised us with a platter of green tea, vanilla, and red bean *mochi*, (yummy ice cream treats), and *sata andagi*, which are basically Japanese donut holes. "To honor Julian," Yujiro said, bowing elegantly. Amaya dipped low, too, her eyes bright with unshed tears, then reached over and hugged me. They've been in America a long time and have learned the art of crossing cultures in style.

Well, while we were enjoying our Japanese-style coffee (pour-over, slow-brewed) and dessert in Julian's honor, I saw Christian signal to Yujiro, who brought another tray to our table, this time one bearing a box wrapped in cherry blossom paper and a red satin bow. Amaya tiptoed along close behind, eyes lit up with anticipation.

"Happy Anniversary, Willow," Christian said, lifting the box from the tray and sliding it over in front of me. Yujiro and Amaya didn't leave, and I realized they were waiting for me to open the gift. Rather curious, indeed. I untied the ribbon and peeled away the paper. Reaching into the box, I withdrew a smoky-blue, wide-mouthed Japanese tea bowl that had clearly been broken and repaired, the cracks filled with what looked like gold in the dim light cast by the subtle ambiance lighting in the restaurant. I didn't completely understand the significance of it and looked around at the three faces watching for my reaction.

"It's beautiful," I murmured. And it was. The repaired seams were perfectly smooth under my fingertips, and although the cracks were organic in nature, the gold filling was so delicate it looked like brush strokes.

Amaya stepped forward, dipped her head respectfully, then explained. "Mr. Goodhope, he gives us the honor to tell you of this Japanese tradition. In Japan, it is called *Kintsugi.* Golden joinery. Sometimes it is called *Kintsukuroi.* Golden repair. When something valuable is broken, we do not throw it away. We gather the pieces, and with the finest material and skill, join them back together to make something beautiful. We do not hide the damage, but fill each crack with shining gold, putting light on the places that are changed." With a fingertip, she traced along one gold fissure, stopping at a spot where a piece of the original blue pottery was completely gone, having been replaced by a similarly shaped piece, but from another dish, with a pink lotus flower on it. "Sometimes not every piece can be found and must be replaced with something else. Perhaps not a perfect match, but something that fills the empty place. Renewal. It is good. The broken places become part of the pattern and are not something to hide." Then she turned to look me square in the face. Beneath the table, Christian's hand rested warm and gentle on my thigh. My tears fell freely.

"Do not hide your broken places, my friend. They are what make you beautiful here." She touched my cheek. "And here." She placed her tiny, slightly gnarled hand over my heart. "Shine a light on the changed places. Let love, love of Julian, and love of your husband be your golden repair."

Willow's Easy Crepes with Elderberry Preserves

Crepes Ingredients
1 Cup All-Purpose Flour
2 Eggs
½ Cup Milk
½ Cup Water
¼ Teaspoon Salt
2 Tablespoons Melted Butter

Cooking Instructions:
(Makes about 8 crepes)
- Whisk together flour and eggs.
- Gradually add milk and water, whisking to combine.
- Add salt and butter, beat until smooth.
- Heat griddle or frying pan over medium heat, lightly oil.
- Pour approximately 1/4 cup of batter onto pan and tilt the pan in a circular motion so batter coats pan bottom evenly.
- Cook for about 2 minutes, flip with spatula, and cook other side for about 2 minutes.

To Serve:
Spread hot crepes with a bit of butter and a thin layer of Elderberry Preserves (see August's recipe for preserves).
Roll crepes up, place seam-side down on plate, add a dollop of whipped cream, and sprinkle with a dash of cinnamon and powdered sugar. YUM!

OCTOBER

October 24th

Dear Mama,

We passed! We passed! We passed! And I've been baking up a storm since I got the go ahead. I took my first order to Mama Dosh on October 6th and she sold out of everything in my basket by noon. It was a huge basket, too, full of a variety of individually-wrapped things, like muffins, scones, coffee cake squares, cookies, tarts, mini pies, donuts, and more. I brought that sampler for the first week, and now her orders are becoming more focused on what people want most: scones (both plain and with elderberries), coffee cake, muffins, and donuts. I'm delivering every weekday—actually, every week night—except Saturday and Sunday. Since I carefully wrap and seal everything, she's fine with me delivering her order in the evening before closing so she has it for the early morning customers. (You'd be amazed at how much wiggle room there is in the term "fresh" when it comes to the food industry.) I don't take her anything on Saturday nights because she's closed on Sundays (which means I have Saturday off!), and on Sunday nights, I only bake a good-sized order of scones, half with, half without elderberries, and deliver it early Monday morning, as in 5 AM! Then I come home and crawl back in bed for another hour or so before waking up to start all over again.

You know me. I'm *not* a morning person.

We have a few kinks to work out. The Monday scone thing isn't ideal for either of us, but it is part of our agreement. That means her Monday customers don't get as many choices, but she's trying to work that whole "scarcity marketing" angle so they'll come back the rest of the week. I know she'd prefer to have her largest selection at the beginning of the week, though, so I'm sure this will have to be dealt with at some point in the near future. I may need to hire someone, but I'm in no position to do so right now, financially, or legally. I'd have to get a whole new slew of paperwork and insurance, etc. How do small businesses like this get past all the red tape before their owner's heads explode????

I've also had some bad baking days—flopped batches, sugary fruit filling bubbling over in the oven and burning, so even the good stuff tastes a little burnt, and had to replace items with other things at the last minute. Mama Dosh is a successful business owner for a reason, and she has high expectations of me. She expects to get what she asks for, not a substitute, and she's always right. The few times I've exchanged cookies for scones or banana muffins for elderberry coffee cake, sales are down. She knows her customers and isn't about to let me get away with special favors. Yes, she's gracious, and she understands I'm in a learning curve right now, but this is her livelihood, and she will do whatever she needs to do to protect that. She did explain to me very clearly, when we worked up our contract, why she wanted to start this as a holiday product. That way, if it flopped, she would be under no obligation to continue carrying my products—we're on a six month probationary period which will carry us well past the holidays and give us a good idea of how well Elderberry Croft goods are being received. She also reminded me that the probationary period is for my benefit, too, that it would give me a much clearer picture of what I'm capable (or not capable) of. She's right about that!

I was under no illusions that it would be smooth sailing from day one, Mama. I mean, the whole idea of cottage industries has always seemed so idealistic to me. The how-to books show ladies in pretty, handmade *clean* aprons with their hair pulled back in perfect braids, make up soft and natural, beatific smiles on their faces. But having worked with you in our little *un*-air conditioned kitchen, in the garden, out foraging, all those years ago, I know it's so not like that in real life, right? Batter splatter on counter tops, stove tops, floors, and even walls on a busy day, dropped berries crushed underfoot (which means I'm tracking little burgundy splotches all over the place), crusty aprons (if I remember to wear one—if not, crusty shirt), permanently berry juice-stained fingers, and certainly no beatific smile on my face. I can see in Christian's eyes when he comes home at the end of the day, secretly wondering if he's going to have elderberry muffins for dinner—again!—or if we're going to have real food, wanting to laugh at the mess I am, but just the smallest bit afraid to, lest I collapse in a heap of tears. It's always the hardest part of the day, because I'm running out of time (and energy!) to make sure the order is complete and ready. I shoot for between 6:00 and 6:30 p.m. drop off time so Christian doesn't have to come home and work more, but he's always ready to jump in and help. Besides, he likes driving for me. Mama Dosh always has big hug and a fresh cup of coffee waiting for him. He's gotten really good at using my uber-sticky plastic wrap. That stuff kills me, Mama. It sticks to itself something awful, and when I'm already in a fluster, I swear the house pixies have jinxed it. Then along comes Christian, with his male model hands and methodical movements, and the stuff just cooperates for him. If it wasn't such a big help at the end of a day, I might be bitter.

I just wasn't expecting her to need so much so quickly, and I have to tell you, I'm exhausted. I get up in the morning, turn on the oven, and start baking. Once things are cool enough, I start packaging. Once things are packaged up, I start gathering things together for making a delivery. Somewhere between all that, I sometimes eat, I sometimes do laundry, and I sometimes bathe. Okay. I shower regularly, but you know what I mean. And now, today, I feel awful. I'm coming down with what's turning into a terrible head cold, but I don't have the option of taking a day off, as it's only Tuesday. I feel like I'm walking around in a bubble. I'm cold, so I pile on the layers, then I'm hot, so I peel everything off then I'm hot again.

I've been drinking a lot of tea, but because I'm not feeling good, I've amped my dose with some elderberry cold and cough syrup, and it seems to help. I'm trying to drink lots of liquids, including homemade chicken soup (I made a big batch last night that should several days). I just can't afford to get sick, but I know it's just because my immune system is overtaxed right now. The long hours, the stress of doing something as a business rather than just for fun, the pressure of making sure everything is uniform and regulated. I'm not sleeping well these days because of wanting so badly to make this happen, and I've had heartburn something fierce form the stress. If I didn't know any better, I'd think I was pregnant, but you don't get a cold from being pregnant. Besides, I wasn't sick at all with Julian. I'm not naive enough to think that all pregnancies are the same, but I'm just sick, that's it.

Which is a little teeny weenie tiny wee bit of a disappointment, I admit. We're starting to talk about having another baby—I think Andrea and George's decision to try again might have triggered a mommy craving in me—but that's all we're doing. Talking about it. No decisions have been made, and I'm beginning to wonder if the only way either of us will feel ready to say 'yes' is to just have it happen. Then the decision will be made for us, and I know we'll both be thrilled.

That being said, if I know we'd both be thrilled over a surprise pregnancy, why are we hesitating to try? Well, I'd love to see this Elderberry Croft business settled in a little more before we have a baby, that's for sure. I don't know how I could possibly manage the hours I'm putting in *and* be a Mommy, too. Princess Baggy already thinks she's been abandoned, poor baby. I moved your robe to a basket right outside the French doors where she can at least see me, but when she starts pacing and crying for me, I hate telling her has to wait. I suppose a baby wouldn't have to sit outside the French doors in a basket, but still....

Oh Mama, reading back, I feel like I've spent the whole letter complaining and how tragic is that! Because here's the thing. I *love* what I'm doing. I *love* what has come out of that year in Elderberry Croft—not just these recipes and this business, but the changes in my heart and the friendships that continue to influence my life—and I *love* that I'm doing something I love from the comfort of the home that I *love*; the home I share with the man that I *love*. I have so much to be thankful for, and every morning, no matter how long my to-do list is, I wake up with a sense of purpose. I may be exhausted, and I may not feel very good. I may look like a harried housewife 95% of the time, but I am a woman loved who is doing what she loves.

The_*Kintsugi* bowl sits in the window over the kitchen sink, filled with a beautiful little cluster of elder flowers. I have been so afraid to put anything in it because I didn't want it to get scratched or stained, but Christian pointed out that the reason it was put back together was so it could be used again. Well, I compromised. They're artificial elder flowers (the trees don't bloom until spring)! There's a craft shop in town that has the most gorgeous silk flowers. I called and asked about elder flowers, the lady (Sarah Jean - doesn't that sound like a flower lady name?) said she'd see what she could do, then she called me back a few days later and told me she had just the thing. And they are, Mama. They look so real I keep expecting to catch a whiff of them every time I wash my hands. I paid dearly for those little umbels, but what better flower to put in my golden repair bowl? All the pieces fit together so beautifully.

There's the timer. I love you, Mama.

Willow's Elderberry Cold and Flu Syrup

Ingredients

3½ Cups of Water

1 Cup Fresh or Frozen or Dried Elderberries

½ Cup Elderflowers

¼ Cup Fresh or Dried Ginger Root (not powder)

2 3-inch Cinnamon Sticks or 2 Teaspoons Ground Cinnamon

1 Teaspoon Whole Cloves or ½ Teaspoon Ground Cloves

1 Cup (or more to taste) Clover or Wildflower Honey (preferably something locally harvested!)

Cooking Instructions:

- Combine all ingredients EXCEPT HONEY in a saucepan and bring to a boil.
- Cover and reduce to a simmer for about 45 minutes to an hour until the liquid has reduced by almost half.
- Remove from heat and let cool enough to be handled. Pour through 2 or 3 layers of cheesecloth (or a fine tea strainer) into a quart-size glass jar.
- Compost or discard pulp and let the liquid cool to lukewarm, then add honey to taste and stir well.
- When honey is well mixed into the elderberry mixture, pour syrup into a pint Mason jar or any clean 16 ounce glass bottle.
- Store in the fridge up to 3 weeks.
- Standard dosages: Kids - about 1 teaspoon every 2-3 hours, Adults - about 1 Tbsp every 2-3 hours.
- Makes a great base for hot tea, too! Simply add 3:1 ratio of hot water to syrup, add more honey to taste, if necessary.

Do NOT add sugar as it suppresses the immune system. I also like to add a slice of fresh lemon when using this syrup as a tea base.

As an Immune Booster During Cold and Flu Season:
Adults take 1 Tablespoon a day, five days a week.
Children take 1 Teaspoon a day, five days a week.

NOVEMBER

November 23rd

Dear Mama,

We're well into November now and I'm finally starting to feel like my old self. The head cold knocked me flat for over a week and I missed out on handing out candy at Halloween. I sate bundled up on the couch in a bunch of blankets while Christian greeted the kids at the door in his Zorro costume. My goodness, he makes a dashing hero. I was almost too miserable to appreciate it. But not quite. Especially after watching a few tittering moms give him the once (twice, thrice) over. Christian, I truly believe, has no clue how delicious he is.

I'm getting into more of the swing of things with my schedule, now that I've been doing this for a month and a half. I can't tell you how much I look forward to weekends, though!

Andrea has been coming over to hang out with me several days a week. She's actually a lot of help, Mama. She's no longer working at the post office, and George is now doing a day shift. He's up for a delivery route position, which is huge for him; for them. Andrea's doing some regular babysitting for a neighbor, and it's enough for now, but they're hoping she can be a stay home mom once their baby comes; she is pregnant, just two months along. We had them over for dinner a few weeks ago to celebrate the lives of their John, whom they lost a year ago, and our Julian, who has been gone two years now. The dinner was a perfect way for us to talk about our boys in a healthy setting, you know?

But during that dinner, a seed was planted in me, and although I haven't said anything anyone, seeing Andrea's enthusiasm and interest in what I'm doing feels like confirmation to me. I think if all goes well with Mama Dosh, if she does want to continue selling my wares, I might be able to offer Andrea a job. It would probably have to start part time, but she could bring her baby with her. It would give me and Christian a reason to open up Julian's room again, to set it up for a baby, even if we aren't ready for one of our own yet. That way, she could still make a little money, and not have to find childcare.

She and George rent a little apartment only a few blocks from her family. They considered moving back to The Coach House, especially when they heard Pru's place was going to be available, but the stream, which is so endearing an element for those living there, is a major deterrent. In fact, they didn't even bother talking to Eddie, but I have a feeling there may be rules in place about people living there with young children. The stream is not fenced and would be almost impossible for any child to resist. Anyway, they like the place they have. It's only one bedroom, but they figure they'll stay there until the baby is at least a year before moving into something bigger. In spite of their somewhat unconventional beginnings, they seem happy and stable.

Neither of them have aspirations for careers or riches, but why should they be? They're very content to focus on home and family, which is lovely in my book.

I have to go pull some pies out of the oven. Mama Dosh has added my elderberry apple pie to her holiday menu and people are gobbling it up. She's had requests for whole pies, but I'm not sure I can keep up if I start taking special orders, too. Maybe next year.

~ ~ ~

November 24th

This coming Thursday is Thanksgiving. Mama Dosh is closed on Thanksgiving, but open on Friday and Saturday, so I'm still going to have to bake. I think I can do some of the stuff on Wednesday and take most of Thursday off from the kitchen, so that will be good. We're going over to Christian's folks for the main meal, and I'm bringing a pumpkin pie and deviled eggs. Nothing with elderberries.

Christian and I stopped by The Coach House after church last Sunday. We'd had lunch with Daddy at Fairhaven so were going by there anyway on our way home. I called Myra to let her know, and she must have let other folks know, because during the hour we were there, almost everyone from the park stopped by to wish us a happy Thanksgiving, some staying to visit. We sat out on her porch and had coffee and oatmeal cookies, and talked about life after Al at The Coach House. Just as Jackson promised, Al's seat is empty... sorta. Myra has turned Al's chair into a plant stand, so now the gorgeous Boston fern Joe and Vivien sent for Al's goodbye party is sitting in it. And yes, everyone walks by it and says, "Hey, Al." But it's not creepy at all. It's—it's just the way of things at The Coach House.

Donny and Shawna have moved into Pru's apartment. I'm still a little surprised no one complained to the landlord, but everyone is just taking it all in stride, as though they're accustomed to Donny's misbehaving. And I suppose they are. They've all been exposed to it repeatedly over the years. From what I can gather, though, Shawna seems to be warming up to folks and I hear in the voices around me that same protective tone they used to have with me. Regardless of what happens to Donny, I think.

While we were there, Doc sidled up to me and asked if I'd care to take a little walk with an old man. Being who he is, he'd already asked Christian's permission, which I thought rather gallant, and I readily agreed. We headed around the driveway toward the other end of the park where his apartment above the garage was, and where, just across the stream, Elderberry Croft sat hidden behind the shrubs and trees lining the water.

Without preamble, he said, "I'm going to Eleanor's for Thanksgiving dinner."

Even though I wanted to jump up and down and squeal like a kid in a candy shop, I respected the fact that he'd pulled me away from the gang to tell me, and I figured this might be something he wasn't ready to share with anyone else. Lest we were being watched, I just reached over, slipped my hand into his, and squeezed. "I'll be praying, Doc. I haven't stopped praying."

"I know, little girl." I'm still Ms. Goodhope to him most of the time, but every once in a while, he calls me 'little girl' like I'm one of his daughters, and it reminds me of that November night a year ago, when he came over and rescued me from myself. I think he thinks I might have done the same for him, but I know better. The changes in Doc's life have been daunting, and he's had to do it pretty much on his own. He's had to choose every day the steps he's going to take to get back home. I may have reminded him what direction to head in, but he's done all the hard work himself. And sometimes, that's the best thing, taking those steps alone. You learn how to walk without using anyone, or anything as a crutch. Yes, he still drinks. Maybe too much; I don't know. But there's a different shine to his eyes, and it's rarely red-tinged the way it used to be. He seems to smile more behind that surprisingly soft beard, too.

He seemed flustered, almost nervous, and it was work to keep from smiling at his obvious uncertainty. "Will this be the first time you've seen each other in a while?"

"Yes. We've got recent pictures of each other. Janeen made us exchange them. The fact Ellie still wants to get together after seeing my picture...." He let his words trail off and patted his chest where he usually keeps his flask. I didn't hear the metallic thunk of it, and realized he had replaced it. He was carrying pictures in his pocket instead, just the way he'd done during the war.

"May I see?" I asked, when he didn't offer. Without hesitation, he slid a photograph from inside his jacket and handed it to me. Oh, Mama. Love is a funny thing. The way Doc said 'Ellie,' you'd think she was some kind of Elizabeth Taylor. But Eleanor is this little butterball of woman with a head of wavy, short, gray hair, silver-framed glasses, and a smile that says 'World's Best Granny." But her eyes. Her eyes are alive, and clear, and sparkle with the youth of a child's. I don't know what Doc sees in that picture of Eleanor, but I see hope, shining bright and clear in those eyes. And in his.

"I'd like to buy one of your pies to take with me, Ms. Goodhope. I promised to bring a dessert, and I'd planned to just grab something from the grocery store on my way out of town, but if you'd do me the honor, I know my girls would love it."

His girls? Is she HIS Eleanor? Oh, I hope so! "You may *have* one of my pies, Doc." My tone careful, I asked, "Is Tracy going to be there, too?"

He nodded, his lips tightening briefly with checked emotion. "Along with her husband, Pete, and my new baby granddaughter, Ruthie."

"Oh, Doc. I'm so glad. I'm so glad for you." I sighed and handed him back his picture. "And I'm so honored you asked for my pie."

That pie is going to be stuffed full of prayers, Mama. I'm making it on Wednesday, and Christian and I will drop it by that night. Eleanor lives about a three hour drive away, so Doc will be heading out early Thursday morning.

Then a weird thing happened. We walked in silence to the bridge, enjoying the crisp November sunshine. But halfway across, I pulled to a stop, suddenly afraid. Suddenly not wanting to see Elderberry Croft. At least not the way it is now. Over this last year, it's slowly, but surely, changed, Mama. Every time I go over there, it's different. It's somehow less. The enchantment is fading, like it's slipping into the shadow lands again. And at that moment, I didn't think I could bear to see it, especially with the memory fresh in my mind of the way it looked last November when Doc and I shared with each other our sad stories in front of the fire pit.

Doc looked at me curiously for a moment or two, then tucked my hand into the crook of his arm, and turned me back the way we came.

"You're the bravest little girl I know, Willow Goodhope. It's all right."

Then I told him my own Thanksgiving secret. Is it wrong that I told him before I told Christian? Before I told you?

Willow's Elderberry-Apple Pie

Ingredients

1 Cup Fresh or 1/2 Cup Dried (reconstituted) Elderberries

3 Tablespoon Cornstarch OR Tapioca

½ Cup White Sugar

1 Tablespoon Lemon Juice

2 ½ Cups Thinly Sliced Tart Apples

2 Teaspoons Ground Cinnamon

¼ Cup Butter

½ Cup Brown Sugar

2 Tablespoons Butter for Under Top Crust

2 Pie Crusts

Cooking Instructions:

- Preheat oven to 375 degrees.
- Press one crust into bottom of 9 or 10-inch pie plate. Bake for 10 minutes or until slightly golden.
- While pie crust is browning, mix cornstarch in a little bit of water (about 1/4 cup – best way to do this is to shake it up in a small jar with a lid.) and add to berries and white sugar. Cook over medium heat, *stirring constantly,* until desired thickness – like syrup. Add more cornstarch if not thick enough. Remove pan from heat, add lemon juice, and set aside.
- Sauté sliced apples in butter and cinnamon, until tender, but not soft. Add brown sugar at the end and toss the apples to coat.
- Gently fold berries into apples. Pour into pie pan, but do not overfill, and reserve any syrup for ice cream later! Place a few pats of butter on top of berries, if desired. Cover with second crust, cut slits or shapes in crust, seal

the edges of the two crusts, and bake at 375 degrees for 30-40 minutes, or until crust is golden brown, and fruit is bubbling up through slits.

Serve with ice cream! Yum.

DECEMBER

December 5th

Christian will be home any minute now. I'm excited and nervous and slightly nauseous with anticipation. My hip-length green sweater looks elegant on my tall frame, but it's so comfortable I feel like I'm in my pajamas. I'm wearing a floor length black knit skirt that covers my socks and bedroom slippers. My feet were cold but I didn't feel like putting on real shoes.

I scan the living room and dining room one more time, the table settings, the candles, the fire burning low in the fireplace, twinkling white lights on our little Christmas tree we just put up yesterday. It's tradition for us to reserve one at a local Christmas tree farm the Saturday after Thanksgiving, then bring it home the first weekend in December and decorate it while drinking eggnog, eating Mexican take-out, and listening to nonstop Christmas music. It's always remarkably romantic. I'd made some special plans for the evening, considering we'd missed out on this two years in a row, having no heart for it the year Julian died, and still living apart last year. We had some making up to do.

We had just strung the lights and plugged them in, standing back to critique our work, when Christian's phone rang. He would have let it go to voicemail if it had been anyone else, but the "Mama Mia" ring tone indicated who it was and he answered it. Before he'd even hung up, Christian was already digging through the jackets on the coat rack.

"Dad fell off the ladder, Willow. He was putting up Christmas lights on the eaves."

"Just now? He was out there putting lights up in the dark?" It wasn't too late, but with the short winter days, it had been full dark for over an hour already. I grabbed my own coat and shrugged into it. It was quite cold for this early in December in our part of the country; a heavy mist hung in the air that felt like a precursor to a storm.

"No." Christian shook his head, clearly frustrated. "It's been almost two hours since he fell. He told Mom he was fine, that he just strained his wrist and needed some ice on it. He wouldn't let Mom take him to the hospital."

"Oh, goodness."

"Yep. And now he's really hurting, and Mom is trying not to panic. I need to go, Willow. I'm sorry." He darted a glance at the tree.

"Oh, goodness," I said again, shoving down the selfish disappointment over the interrupted evening. "*We* need to go. I'm coming, too, silly. Our little tree will wait until tomorrow. Or next weekend. Come on."

It was after midnight when we left the hospital, and delivered Christian's parents to their own place, making sure his dad was comfortable, his broken wrist in a shiny new cast propped on a pile of pillows in bed. Charlotte, grateful for our help, apologized profusely for keeping us out so late. We assured her she'd done the right thing in calling us, then headed for home ourselves. We went straight to bed, exhausted, and both anticipating early Monday mornings ahead of us. In spite of the late hour, Christian lay awake for a while, tense and restless, admittedly worried about his dad. "Not just because of the broken arm, Willow, but because he didn't have the good sense to go to the doctor. That's what worries me most. What if he'd been alone? If Mom had been out for the evening?"

I understood, and kept my own emotional upheaval over all that had happened to myself. He didn't need anything else on his plate at that moment. Besides, sleep was dragging me under and I knew I wouldn't be coherent much longer. "I know, Christian. But that little doctor gave him the what for, and I have a feeling it scared Dad enough that he might think twice the next time something like this happens." I regretted the words as soon as they were out. "If there is a next time, I mean. We'll just pray there isn't." I fell asleep to the quiet timbre of my husband's voice. I think he was doing just that; praying.

It had been rough getting up less than four hours later to deliver my scones to Cafe Siena, but I did it with a smile, made it back home in record time, crawled under the covers next to the very warm body of my snoring husband, and promptly fell back to sleep. I didn't wake again until my alarm went off at 9:00 a.m. I'd given myself an extra hour of sleep after all the night's shenanigans. I was becoming more comfortable with my baking schedule and was no longer waking up quite so anxious. I knew the extra hour of sleep would pay off in the long run.

I did get straight to work, though, barely taking time for a couple cups of coffee and a leftover scone or two from this morning's delivery. I wanted to be done early, deliver my order before Christian got home, and do all I could to make up for last night's disrupted evening.

I don't want to wait until next weekend to finish the little party for two we started last night. The tree still needs decorating, there's still eggnog to drink, and we still have some Christmas music to dance to.

The pork loin roast is coming out in about thirty minutes—that should give Christian enough time to shower if he wants to before we eat. I've been marinating that thing in olive oil, lemon juice, garlic, and a bunch of herbs since I got out of bed this morning, and my mouth is watering just thinking about it. Twice baked potatoes, a big salad, rosemary bread sticks, and tender julienned green beans that I'll sauté last minute.

I hear his car. I press my cool palms to my flushed cheeks. Will it always be like this? Oh, may it be so!

I hurry to the door to greet him, and he's ushered in on a gust of wind, the collar of his long coat standing up around his neck against the damp December chill, his nose and cheeks red. He deposits his briefcase on the foyer bench as I unbutton the lapels of his coat and slip inside it. Wrapping my arms around his waist, I press my body to the length of his, sharing with him my warmth.

"Mm. You feel good," he murmurs into my hair, pulling me close. I lift my face to his and he kisses me, his lips cold against mine, making me gasp and pull away. His hands are like ice as he grabs my face and draws me back for more, threading his fingers into my hair, kneading the warm ridges at the back of my neck. "You smell good, too," he says against my mouth.

"So do you," I murmur, when he finally comes up for air. I breathe in the clinging scent of his job—wood paneling, lemon furniture polish, paperwork, and coffee—the faded notes of his cologne and the man-smell of his skin as I bury my face in his neck. I press my cheek to the contrasting textures of the lapels of his suit over his smooth white cotton shirt. His tie is already gone, something he ritually does as soon as he puts the car in park in our driveway. I know if I dig in his coat pockets, I'll find the tie with whichever *Dr. Who* tie pin he chose to wear this morning still attached, along with a few coins, his work pass, and his blue tooth, the accoutrements of his trade. Christian loves his career choice, but he's still bottom man on the totem pole, and he's more than happy to shelve (or pocket) the burdens of his work before setting foot inside the house.

It still sometimes catches me by surprise to see him come through that door in suit and tie. He's always been kind of a classy guy, but up until he landed this job, the suits were special occasion wear only. That little jolt is one of sheer pleasure, though. He's very handsome with his ebony hair and hint-of-olive skin, and those suits on him make me think of those casually posed male models on high fashion magazine covers. I'm sure there's a branch of Black Irish or Spaniard somewhere in his family tree. All we know for sure, though, is our last name, Goodhope, sprang from his family's early American Quaker roots, a far cry from *Dolce & Gabanna* photo shoots.

There's nothing Quaker about the way his hands are sliding up under my sweater now, his cold fingers brushing against the bare curve of my back. I make a startled noise and squirm against him, which only makes him laugh, the sound rumbling against my cheek. "It's good to come home to you, wife."

In those words, I not only hear the truth of what he

means today, but the reality of what it was like when I wasn't here to come home to. I refuse to go back there, though. I refuse to pick up that cloak of shame again. And Christian would feel terrible if he thought his words invoked me to do so.

"You're not just coming home to me tonight," I say, without thinking how that might sound. He takes a quick step back, his eyes darting around for any sign of company, and I have to laugh. "No, no. It's just us. I just meant I've got a real dinner in the oven for us, not burnt muffins."

"So," he pulls me back up against him and rasps his jaw over mine. "We *are* alone, then? I can ravish you right here in the front entry and no one will be offended?"

I laugh out loud—cackle, chortle, whatever that noise is I make—put both hands flat against his chest, and push. "I might be offended if you make me burn the pork loin."

He grins and says something under his breath about heat and loins. I can't tell if my face is burning more from his words or from his stubble.

"No more kissing until you shave, 5 O'clock Shadowman." I tentatively touch my face with my fingertips. "Ow."

He eyes the redness and smirks, as if to say, *Yep. My manliness did that.* Sometimes I think he gets a kick out of marking me that way, knowing it will fade away shortly. Is that a guy thing? Like marking his territory? I roll my eyes at him and he nods. I swear that man can read my mind.

"Go," I tell him, turning toward the kitchen, my skirt swirling sensually around my calves. A current of electricity buzzes just beneath my skin, and I have to force myself not to look at him, lest I lose track of the plans I have for the evening. "Dinner is ready in fifteen minutes," I call over my shoulder, then I pull the French doors closed behind me.

I'm dishing up our plates when he saunters into the kitchen and eyes me up and down, his gaze stopping on my tingling jaw line, still red, I'm certain. He's clearly feeling no less frisky than when he first walked in the front door, but looking much more comfortable, dressed in jeans and a blue and gray flannel shirt, unbuttoned over a black t-shirt. He's showered, I can tell by the damp tendrils of hair curling at his neckline, and shaved, and applied a fresh splash of cologne. That's good if he's expecting another make-out session any time soon; my skin can't handle the scruff.

"Sorry about your pretty face, baby." He steps up close behind me, gently pulling my back against him, and nuzzles my neck with his now smooth chin, planting light kisses along the unscathed side of my jaw. His eyes move to the plates in my hand. "That looks amazing." His voice deepens and he growls in my ear. "I'm ravenous."

I turn in his arms, a plate still in each hand, and kiss him hard. "Later," I promise. "We eat first."

I have him grab the salad plates and we head out to the little dining room where I've already set the table, complete with tall-stemmed goblets, fancy napkins, and forks for every course. In the center of the table, between two slender candles, I've placed the *Kintsugi* tea bowl with its silk elder flowers on a cake pedestal under a glass dome. The candle light flickers with every move we make, turning the centerpiece into something straight out of a fairytale.

"So what's the occasion?" he asks after he blesses the food for us.

"I tried a new Christmas cake recipe and I needed a guinea pig. I figured you were getting so tired of elderberry products that I'd have to bribe you with meat and potatoes first."

He grins at me, clearly waiting for more. I cut a good size bite of pork and stick it in my mouth, chewing carefully, my throat dry.

"It must be some cake." He spears a pearled onion and holds it up. "You never serve me onions on purpose."

"Oh, it is. It's an eggnog spice cake with elderberry glaze. Eggnog, Christian. Eggnog! You know it's going to be divine." I smile brightly, feeling my face flush under his scrutiny, then lower my eyes to the onion still held aloft on his fork. "Besides, last night didn't go quite the way I—we planned. I thought this might be a nice way to make up for it." I hope the flickering light cast by the candles hides my pink cheeks.

"Willow." He puts the fork down. Without eating the prized onion.

"What? You don't like my cooking tonight?" I shove another bite into my mouth, concentrating very hard on cutting my pork into perfectly square pieces.

"Willow." He slides his chair back just a little. Something in his voice makes me look up sharply. The sensual teasing tone is gone; he sounds like he might be choking.

"What's wrong?" I ask, practically dropping my fork, hearing it clatter noisily against my china plate. He doesn't look so good, all pale around the gills, and he doesn't seem to be breathing. The Heimlich maneuver! Am I going to have to do the Heimlich on my husband? Can I even remember how to do it? Through my mind flashes the image of a heavily mustached German man in *lederhosen* laughing at my terrible life-saving efforts while my husband flops around in my arms.

Where did *that* come from? Besides, Dr. Heimlich was an

American physician. And he was bald. And I don't think he even had a mustache. Or *lederhosen*, for that matter! I shake my head to clear it of this ridiculous rabbit trail. "Are you choking? Can you take a drink, honey?"

I reach for his water glass, but the bulky fabric of my sweater sleeve brushes up against my own full one, knocking it over, sending a surge of ice-cold water across the table, diverging around his plate, over the edge of the table, and into his lap.

Christian leaps to his feet, almost sending his chair over backward, and I let out a startled squawk. Princess Baggy, who's been curled in a ball of bliss on mom's bathrobe in her kitty bed, scrabbles to her feet as well, hissing, back arched. I push my own chair back, making it screech over the tile floor, apologizing profusely to my stunned husband, and the terrified cat dashes into the living room and straight up the trunk of the Christmas tree, which then which topples over in spite of its wide plastic base, the water from the basin making a wide puddle on the carpet beneath the downed tree. The little white lights flicker once, twice, then with the sound of a cork being released, all the remaining lights in the living room and dining room go out.

Princess Baggy careens down the hall in the dark, presumably seeking refuge in our bedroom. In the flickering glow of the two candles still bravely burning on the table between us, I can just make out the stunned look on my husband's face. The fire in the fireplace has burned down to embers and offers no light from across the room.

I open my mouth to speak, feel a giggle clambering up the back of my throat, but within moments of breaking free, the laughter turns to tears. This is not how I envisioned this going. Not at all.

I feel for my chair and drop heavily into it, my face in my hands. And then I'm crying for real and I don't understand why. This should be funny. Any other time this whole thing would have had me belly laughing like a hyena. But now, sitting here in the dark, having doused my hot-blooded husband with frigid water, my carefully laid plans being foiled not once, but two nights in a row, after all my hard work to make this a night to remember.

Behind my hands, between sobs, I say, "I—I'm pregnant."

And then he's there, kneeling in front of me, his long arms reaching around me, pulling me close. He presses his cheek to my flat stomach, barely breathing, and I lower my hands to his head, running my fingers through his hair. He's got such lovely hair, inky in the candle light, thick, but soft to touch.

"Are you sure?" he whispers.

"Yes. Absolutely sure. He or she is about the size of a bean already."

His arms tighten briefly, he pulls back just a little, then murmurs, "Hi, Bean. It's me, your daddy."

Straightening, he brings his hands up to cup my face. My eyes are adjusting to the dim light and I can see the tears in his, too. "Thank you," he says, before leaning in to kiss me, deeply, thoroughly.

Sometime later, we're sitting on blanket on the floor in front of a blazing fire. Our bellies are full of good food, the little Christmas tree is upright and showing no signs of distress, decked out in all its Christmas finery, Princess Baggy curled in a ball on my lap. I hand Christian the *Kintsugi* bowl and explain how the night was supposed to go.

"As soon as the dishes were cleared, I was going to ask you to take that out of the cake stand to make room for the cake. You were supposed to look down at it and that's when I'd tell you, if you couldn't figure it out by those tiny socks." I point to the fuzzy white bumps poking up through the lacy umbels. "It was such great symbolism, too. The whole golden repair and new life and our new baby."

"I'm sorry, Willow." He's trying not to smile. He's been trying not to crack up all night long. "I'm not sorry about the way things went, because honestly, I don't think I'll ever forget this night." I would elbow him if Princess Baggy wasn't sound asleep on my lap. I feel terrible about scaring her so badly and I refuse to do anything to startle her now. He carefully plucks the baby socks from the middle of the flowers and sets the bowl on the floor behind him. Toying with them, he continues. "But I am sorry that you didn't get to do things in a way that would make you happy."

I look over at him. "But I am happy. And look at us. This is perfect. It all turned out perfectly."

"Well, once I'd gotten out of those ice pants, things did get considerably better." He winks, and I smile back at him, hoping he can see how completely sated I feel right now. Leaning forward, he kisses the tip of my nose, then pushes up to his feet. "I'll be right back. I have a gift for you, too."

I'm pleasantly surprised, and wait patiently for him to return, and when he does, he's holding an object wrapped in one of his shirts. I look up at him with raised eyebrows when he holds it out to me.

"I don't know where the wrapping paper is. I figured this is the ultimate in recycling and you'd be proud of me." He taps the object. "Wrapping paper you can wear."

"Very functional," I nod in agreement, beginning to peel up the strips of Scotch tape he's plastered all over the thing.

From the folds of the shirt, I withdraw a gorgeous leather

bound notebook with a leather thong tied around it to keep it closed. "Oh Christian. This is incredible."

"Open it up," he insists, taking the shirt from me and crumpling it in a ball between his large hands. He almost seems nervous.

Untying the thong, I let the book fall open in my hands, then begin to thumb through the empty pages. It feels completely handmade, from the leather tooling on the cover to the roughened fibers of the paper. Then my eye catches a glimpse of Christian's script near the front, and I turn there, anxious to read what he's written. But he reaches over and gently pressed the book closed before I can.

"No, wait," he says. "Let me explain first, then you can read it." He is nervous. I reach over and lace my fingers through his. "I know you've been writing to your mom, Willow. Don't worry," he hurries to assure me in response to my eyes widening in surprise. "I haven't read your letters. But," he takes a deep breath. "I want you to think about something, Willow. The point of letters is to correspond with each other, right? I write to someone, they respond to my questions or anecdotes with some of their own, right?"

He waits for me to nod in agreement.

"Well, obviously, your mom isn't going to write you back."

"No, but I feel like I know what her letters might be like if she could." My voice sounds a little defensive, even though I don't mean it to. "But you're right."

"Here's the thing. I know of someone who loves you just as much, if not more, than your mother, someone who not only would write you back, but would cherish every single letter you ever wrote." He drops his gaze to the book on my lap, his one hand still resting flat on the closed cover, the other squeezing my fingers in a cadence matching my pulse.

"You want me to write to you?" My question is really not necessary. Of course that's what he's asking.

"Yes. I have written you a letter in this journal, Willow, and I want you to write back to me. And then I'll write back to you, and we'll keep going back and forth, back and forth." His voice is low, but fervent, then he ducks his chin so he can look me in the eye. "I want you to pour your heart out to me, Willow."

I dip my head, the truth of what he's saying dawning on me. He believes I've withheld those pieces of me from him, those things I could say to my mother, but maybe not to him. Is he right?

After only a moment or two, I shake my head firmly in answer to my own searching. Christian has my whole heart. Every piece. Every shard. Every jagged edge, every perfect pattern. He has it all and I give it to him freely. Maybe at some point, he might have been right, but not anymore. He holds the pieces of my heart together in the golden joinery of his love.

I lift my shining eyes to him, nod, and whisper, "I will." Those words, the same words I'd spoken years ago, in front of all our family and friends, in response to the pastor asking me to promise to love and cherish my husband. Those words so few, yet so important, so small, yet like refined gold, strong enough to join us together forever.

I slide the journal out from under his hand and open it again to the first page. My heart leaps at the sight of my name, so elegantly scrawled across the first line, as though he's breathed part of himself into the ink that covers the page with words from his heart to mine.

~ ~ ~

Dear Mama,

Thank you for being who you are, for helping me to be the person I am.

Thank you for teaching me how to be a woman, a lover, a wife, a mother, a friend. For teaching me how to embrace the people God gives me to share my life with.

Thank you for teaching me to choose life.

Hug Julian for me. Take care of each other, okay? I love you, Mama. I always will.

The End

Willow's Eggnog Spice Christmas Cake

With Elderberry Glaze

Ingredients

3 Cups Flour

1 Teaspoon Baking Powder

½ Teaspoon Salt

2 Teaspoons Ground Cinnamon

1 Teaspoon Freshly Grated Nutmeg

½ Teaspoon Ground Allspice

¼ Teaspoon Ground Cloves

1 Cup Softened Butter

2 Cups White Sugar

½ Cup Brown Sugar

6 Eggs

1 Cup Refrigerated or Canned Eggnog

2 Teaspoons Vanilla

Elderberry Glaze

1 Cup Sifted Powdered Sugar

2 Teaspoons Elderberry Syrup

2 Tablespoons Whipping Cream

Cooking Instructions
- Heat oven to 350 degrees.
- Generously grease and flour a 12-cup Bundt pan; set aside.
- Combine dry ingredients (first 7 ingredients) and set it aside.
- Beat butter at medium speed with an electric mixer until creamy.

- Gradually add white sugar first, then brown sugar, beating 5 to 7 minutes, until butter and sugar mixture is creamy again.
- Add eggs, 1 at a time, beating on low speed just until yellow disappears.
- Add vanilla.
- Add dry ingredients and eggnog to butter mixture alternately, a little at a time.
- Beat at low speed just until blended after each addition.
- Bake at 350 degrees for 50 - 55 minutes or until a long toothpick comes out clean. (Be sure to stick toothpick down to middle of cake.)Cool in the pan on a wire rack for about 15 minutes, then remove cake from pan and let it cool another 10 - 15 minutes until cool to the touch.
- Combine glaze ingredients, stirring until smooth.
- Drizzle glaze over cake and serve!

A Note from Becky

Dear Reader,

I hope you enjoyed the journey home with Willow Goodhope. And I'd love to hear from you if you tried any of Willow's elderberry recipes!

I like to say I write HOPE-fully ever afters. Hopefully ever after because real life isn't always wrapped up in a pretty pink bow, is it? I write fiction about real-life people and real-life situations. Because we love to escape into our fiction, but we want that escape to resonate with us, right?

If you're looking for fiction with relatable characters, relevant situations, and redemptive storylines, I invite you to check out some of my other books and series. You may meet your next BFF (Best Fiction Friend)! Or visit me online: BeckyDoughty.com.

I write heartfelt and wholesome Contemporary Romance, Romantic Suspense, and Women's Fiction. I write fiction, mainly because nonfiction is hard! Yes, I've tried. Let's just say I like to color outside the lines when it comes to facts. But emotions and feelings and the roller coaster ride that comes with all relationships? Oh yeah. That's where you'll find me.

Where hope lives and love wins. Every single time.

~ Becky Doughty

An excerpt...

THE GOODBYE GIRL

Pemberton Manor Book 1

"Wait up! Please!"

The man standing at the back of the old fashioned lift just stared at me as I careened through the small lobby, two bulging canvas grocery bags slung over my shoulder and dragging my overloaded luggage trolley behind me.

"Thanks for your help," I muttered under my breath as I turned and wedged myself through the narrow opening. I wasn't worried about him picking up on my sarcasm; earbud cords hung down either side of his neck and disappeared inside the collar of his coat. But I was so relieved there was someone else riding up with me that I didn't care. It was Christmas Eve, for Saint Nick's sake, and I wasn't going to let some rude guy in an elevator get to me.

Okay. It wasn't an elevator. Not by a long shot. As far as I was concerned, it barely qualified as a lift. An ancient Otis manual traction elevator, it was operated by a hand crank set into one wall of the cab...move the lever clockwise to go up, counterclockwise to go down, bring it to 12 o'clock to stop. And it was not self-leveling. It took a bit of finesse to line the bottom of the lift up with whatever floor you were stopping at.

The first time I'd braved it—and only after Sarah's relentless badgering—it had gotten stuck just past the second floor. My sister had laughed at my mini panic and casually slid open the accordion cage door and then slammed it shut again, latching it back into place. "Sometimes it does that," she explained as I stared in horror at the gaping opening between the threshold of the lift and the brick wall of the shaft.

"What if I got my leg stuck in there right as the thing started up again?" I asked, horrified at the grisly images that flooded my over-active imagination. "How can this thing even be legal?"

Sarah rolled her eyes. "You sound like one of my kids. Always suggesting the most improbable scenarios." She eyed me over her shoulder as she slid the door latch in place before reaching for the crank again. "Not only would your leg not even fit in there, Gracie, but why on earth would you put it in there in the first place?"

She had a point, but thankfully, I didn't have to acknowledge her superior reasoning skills because the elevator had responded with a clank and a shudder, and then lurched its way up the shaft until Sarah brought it to a stop in perfect position at the third floor level. The screeching of the sliding door grated against my nerves, and for just a moment, I experienced a visceral sympathy for domesticated birds living in their pretty little cages. I clamped my teeth together and didn't say another word as I waited for her to push open the security door to let us out.

The security door that supposedly kept folks from tumbling to their deaths into the shaft when the elevator was on a different floor.

"Why do you even take this thing if it gets stuck all the time?" I ventured to ask her.

"It doesn't get stuck all the time, only every once in a while. And then you just have to reset it. No big deal." Maybe no big deal to her, but her brain didn't work the way mine did. "Besides, there's just something about this old Otis; it's one of the reasons I chose to rent an apartment here. I think it gives Pemberton Manor character, don't you?"

Character or not, here I was, launching myself back into the leg-crushing death trap, this time with someone who clearly couldn't care less about the fact that I might be a bit of a nervy co-passenger. In fact, he looked right past me, as though I wasn't even worth the effort to acknowledge. Must be some good music he was listening to.

The cheesy old Aerosmith song popped into my head against my will, making me feel even more uncomfortable, but I consoled myself with the certainty that there would be no love lost in this elevator.

I smiled politely at the guy anyway—he didn't smile back—and then realized I'd effectively boxed him in and now I would have to be responsible for operating the lift. I spun around, a brief futile hope rising up in me that the brass plated crank mechanism had been upgraded to a backlit numbered panel....

"Oh!" I said as I took in the tiny woman in the corner and the even tinier little girl at her side. Her tiny little girl hands gripped the crank and her tiny little girl face was lit up with anticipation. The only thing that wasn't tiny about the duo was the woman's belly bulging out from the front of her unbuttoned coat. She looked like she was due to give birth at any moment.

The woman's hand on the girl's shoulder wasn't resting there lightly, I noticed. If not for the child's puffy jacket, she might have left bruises with her white-knuckled grip. I forced my mouth to soften into a gentler smile than the one I'd given the guy, but the woman spared me only a quick glance before shifting her gaze back to the floor at her feet.

Was she all right? In pain? Oh God. Was she in labor?

Please let us not get stuck tonight! The thought raced through my head.

"Is this it?" I asked, my words bursting out of my mouth in feigned excitement the way Sarah's did when she was trying to get the attention of all twenty-one of her first grade students. I cleared my throat and tried again in a calmer, more non-teacher tone. "Are we waiting for anyone else?"

"Nope!" the child declared in her tiny little girl voice, bouncing up and down on her tiny little girl toes—or at least I assumed they were, since they were hidden inside tiny little girl ladybug rain boots. "Let's go, let's go, let's go!"

I swallowed hard and looked away; every time she bounced, her head bumped against her mother's belly

Please don't pop. Please don't pop. Please don't pop.

I looked over my shoulder at the man who was now studying a section of the decorative molding that ran along the top of the paneled walls of the cab. Apparently, he hadn't heard my question.

"Sir?" I said a little louder, resisting the urge to jerk one of the speakers from his ears. "Are you waiting for anyone else?" Why I'd taken it upon myself to make sure no one else was joining us, I had no idea. Maybe I was subconsciously hoping I'd have to get off the lift to make room.

The man turned and met my eyes, albeit only briefly, but then in a quiet voice replied, "I am not," before looking beyond me again. What was with these people and the whole no-eye-contact thing?

"Well." And once again, I was channeling Sarah. Her chipper voice inside my head bolstered me, however, and I needed all the courage I could amass at the moment. "I'm not quite sure how to do this, but there's a first time for everything, right?" I reached for the handle of the cage door and began to tug on it.

It didn't budge.

"You ha'ta lock the other door and push the button on the floor first," said the child, who couldn't have been more than four or five years old. "Want me to show you?"

I glanced at the girl's mother for cues, but the woman just withdrew her hand from her daughter's shoulder and rested back against the wood-paneling behind her.

"Careful, Itsy," she said, her voice husky, not like a smoker's, but like that of someone who didn't speak a lot. There were dark circles under her eyes and the slump of her shoulders led me to believe she was taking the elevator because she might just be too weary to take the stairs today. Although the child appeared well cared for with her rosy cheeks and shiny blond hair, the bones in the woman's face seemed too close to the surface, and her hands, now folded over her distended belly, showed no signs of late pregnancy weight gain or water retention. She looked too skinny to be healthy. Was it just a difficult pregnancy? Or worse?

A creepy sci-fi movie I'd watched with my brothers years ago flashed through my mind. In it, aliens came to earth to live in peace among humans, but to their dismay, their babies kept dying before they were born. Through a series of ridiculously contrived circumstances, the aliens discovered that if their babies had humans as surrogate mothers, they acclimated to life on earth. The movie got weird then because the combination of healthy human prenatal care and advanced alien development created these alien super babies that got a little too aggressive *in utero*. They essentially turned into little parasites that ate their way out of their surrogates…

I coughed and swallowed hard, willing away the mental images, but when I saw the woman's belly twitch and roll under her laced fingers, I looked away quickly and focused instead on Itsy. She clearly was no alien super baby, but a sweet normal human child.

Itsy. For some reason, the name delighted me. Was it a *Fried Green Tomatoes* reference? An "Itsy Bitsy Spider" tribute? Short for something like Isabella or Elisabeth? Wherever it derived from, it fit the diminutive child perfectly, and I grinned down at her. "Sure. Why don't you show me how the door works."

I bit back the warning to make sure she didn't get her leg stuck in the gap.

Itsy instructed me on how to make certain the safety door was latched first, and then squatted and pointed at the foot release on the floor at the edge of the threshold. "Step on that button first. Then you can close the pretty door."

The pretty door. Not a label I'd use to describe the bars that would lock us in. I wondered if the mother and child had ever gotten stuck inside the old Otis.

"Got it," I said and waited until Itsy had popped back up and stepped away before I slid my foot forward. I hesitated briefly, giving only a moment's air time to the vision of me pushing the lever the wrong way and sending us all plummeting to our deaths. Then I squared my shoulders, pressed down on the foot release mechanism, and slid the metal cage shut.

"Can I turn the handle now?" Itsy asked, bouncing in place again. At her mother's nod, she applied herself to the task with great concentration, the tiny tip of her tongue protruding from between her pursed lips.

She took us down first. I hadn't even been aware there was a basement in the old place.

My oldest sister lived on the third floor of a stately, 100-year-old home that had been converted into apartment living sometime in the last twenty or thirty years. Pemberton Manor was one of many old Victorians in our area that had met such a fate. Midtown residents took great pride in their city with its prestigious Southern California University, the registered historical district and quaint downtown, the open air amphitheater that housed class-act performances every summer, the meandering streets that marked the routes for annual bicycle races and marathons, and so much more. But over the last several years, Midtown had seen a surge of growth and development, which meant the old blue bloods had to make way for the up-and-comers with their hybrid transportation and dual-income-no-kids lifestyles. Now, instead of these old converted Victorians housing college students who opted to live off campus, more often than not, the studio apartments were being filled with renters like Sarah who had steady jobs and no plans to move anytime soon in the foreseeable future.

I supposed the owners of places like Pemberton Manor were fine with that—they didn't have to worry about finding new renters every semester, or having to clean up after university students who saved up their laundry for summer vacation. But every time I stepped foot inside Pemberton Manor, I couldn't help feeling just a little bit sorry for the old dame. At one time, I imagined she'd been a tall and elegant beauty with her gabled windows and sharply angled roof lines, the spindled balconies and wide covered porch. But now, the house just felt weary to me. Tired. Not quite taken care of the way she once was. Too many people coming and going, taking bits and pieces of her soul with them, and leaving less and less of her behind.

It didn't help that the maintenance guy, Sean Something-or-other, didn't maintain much of anything around the place. Sean lived on the property in a detached converted garage, and Sarah insisted he had to be a distant relative of the homeowner. There was no other explanation for him being able to keep the job he never performed. She only called him when she was in dire straits and couldn't figure out how to repair something by Googling it. Those calls typically ended with her contacting a professional—at Sean's advice, of course—which is the only reason she even called him in the first place. If he recommended a professional, then it was paid for by the landlord.

The Otis elevator jolted to a stop and Itsy cried out, "B is for basement!"

Itsy's mother clapped softly, so I joined in. After a few moments of uncomfortable silence while Itsy beamed at the oblivious man in the corner, I added encouragingly, still using my Sarah voice, "That's right. And what floor are you and your mommy going to tonight?"

"Three!" she proclaimed, and I clapped with much greater enthusiasm.

<< >>

Want to read the rest of Grace's story for free?
Subscribe to Becky Doughty's Reader News at BeckyDoughty.com

<< >>

Made in the USA
Las Vegas, NV
21 October 2020